Gordon S. Dickson was born near Inverness, Scotland, but left there soon after when the family returned to Northern Ireland, where he still resides. He was educated at Secondary and Grammar schools, and scraped through English 'O' level, as essay writing was not a strong point. He was employed in the Civil Service for a number of years and is now retired. He has only recently taken up writing. He enjoys reading, gardening, watching football, and occasional visits to the cinema.

Other books by this author

Verdict Unknown
Verdict Unknown...the Sequel
The Sheriff of River Bend
Des Pond, Special Agent

3 Bartonshire Tales:
The Wartime Adventures of Harry Harris
An Impossible Quest
The Heir...Apparently + Ashes to Ashes

The Life and Times of Victoria-Ann Penny
The Spanish Armada...What if it all went wrong?

To Ben, who is a Burton Albion fan.
Also an Arsenal fan... but no one is perfect!

Gordon S. Dickson

DETECTIVE INSPECTOR
DENISON STORIES

The Imposter and the
Informers' Murders

AUSTIN MACAULEY PUBLISHERS™

LONDON • CAMBRIDGE • NEW YORK • SHARJAH

A CIP catalogue record for this title is available from the British Library.

ISBN 9781398477094 (Paperback)
ISBN 9781398477100 (ePub e-book)

www.austinmacauley.co.uk

First Published 2024
Austin Macauley Publishers Ltd®
1 Canada Square
Canary Wharf
London
E14 5AA

The Imposter

Chapter One

Friday, January 13th

The headline in the early edition of the "Castlewood Herald and Advertiser" read:

'TWO BODIES RECOVERED FROM RIVER TRENT.'

(A photograph of two bodies covered in sheets appeared below this)

'Police have recovered two bodies, one male and one female, from the River Trent yesterday (Thursday) evening. Three boys discovered the bodies approximately two miles downriver from Castlewood city centre. Foul play is suspected.

'Police reports indicate that both victims were police officers who had been reported missing since last Tuesday (tenth inst.). The next of kin have been informed by the police. We will bring you further information as it is disclosed.'

***

The two deceased officers were Detective Sergeant Gwen Travis and Detective Constable John Savage, both in their twenties and highly respected in the local constabulary. Their colleagues in Castlewood Police Headquarters were deeply shocked when the bodies were found, though they had suspected foul play was involved in their sudden disappearance. The last couple of days had seen extensive searches conducted.

The two officers had been making enquiries in the Edward Street area of the city regarding the disappearance of a young local woman.

Castlewood Criminal Investigation Department (C.I.D.) had received special permission to investigate the deaths of the officers, which would normally have been awarded to detectives unconnected to the victims, because a spate of murders and terrorist incidents had tied up all other nearby C.I.Ds. Fortunately, Castlewood had escaped any terrorist attacks.

***

Friday, January 13th in the afternoon

Officers immediately recommenced door-to-door enquiries in the area where the two officers were last known to be operating: Edward Street and the nearby cathedral precincts.

'Excuse me, sir, may we have word with you?' a detective asked a man in clerical garb.

'Yes, of course,' replied the man, Dean Hopgood of St John's Church of England Cathedral, Castlewood-upon-Trent, in the county of Staffordshire, England.
A friendly rivalry existed between St John's, Castlewood, a sturdy Norman building with a large square tower at the centre of the crossing, and the nearby mediaeval "English Gothic" style cathedral of St Chad and St Mary, Lichfield, with its

three graceful sandstone spires. These were nicknamed "The Three Maidens in the Vale": a landmark visible for miles.

It was unusual in the Church of England to have two cathedrals in such close proximity, but a historical quirk in the dioceses' boundaries placed the two cathedrals only ten miles apart. King Henry VIII had created a new bishopric in Castlewood to reward a friend.

'I am Detective Inspector Walter Denison of Castlewood C.I.D.,' the detective resumed, presenting his warrant card. 'This is Detective Sergeant Mary Loan.' He indicated his colleague. 'Are you Dean Hopwood, Dean Harold Hopwood?'

'Yes, but it is Hopgood, with a *g*,' the dean replied with a smile.

'I apologise. It's my poor writing,' said the inspector glancing at his notebook to make a correction. He took a pencil from a pocket, checked the lead was adequate with a quick lick and made a correction.

'No problem, Inspector. My writing is terrible, too,' the dean grinned. 'Always has been since my school days.'

To say Detective Inspector Walter Trevor Denison was as broad as he was tall might be an exaggeration, but only a slight one. Aged forty, he stood five feet five inches in his socks and had a large waistline. His trousers' waistband had received several inserts sewn by his devoted wife, Millicent. They had been married for more than twenty years. Denison loved his food! Millicent was an excellent cook. 'That's why I married you,' Denison often joked. Her response shall remain unwritten.

He was prematurely bald since his late twenties, with just a combover remaining. He had dark blue eyes and large ears. Colleagues joked about elephants…when he was not around, of course! What could be described as a "Clark Gable" moustache inhabited the space under his nose. 'A plus with the ladies,' Denison often said jokingly! His wife just shook her head. *The only resemblance between you and Clark Gable is that you are both male,* she thought but never said. She just smiled sweetly.

Detective Sergeant Mary Loan was the opposite. Originally from Salford, Greater Manchester, she was slim, nearly six feet tall, aged thirty, had long blonde hair in a ponytail, and deep brown eyes. She excelled at sports and was on the Staffordshire County Police Force's ladies' basketball and tennis teams. She was wearing a dark red coat with a fake fur collar and a white scarf against the winter cold.

'Yes, I am the dean. At least that is why they pay me,' the dean continued with a smile.

'We are here on a rather serious matter, sir,' said Denison. The dean nodded feeling rebuked. 'The bodies of two of our colleagues have been found a mile or so downriver from here. They were in this area investigating the disappearance of a young woman,' said Denison.

'I know; I heard the bodies had been found. It is terrible, shocking. The young woman they were enquiring about lived close to here. But how does it connect with me?' asked the dean.

'Not you personally, sir, but they were last reported to be interviewing people in this area. This was last Tuesday, the tenth of January.'

'Oh yes, I did notice two people in the area late in the evening. It was dark and cold. I had been to a seminar, a rather tedious seminar I might add, in London that day, so they must have missed me. I went straight indoors for my dinner as it was bitterly cold, and I was starving. It is a long drive, even on the motorway. I hate eating in motorway restaurants. So expensive! Even a cup of coffee is double the normal price.

'My wife and I have a little house in the cathedral close.' It was really a large, detached house which came with the office of Dean.

The "close" was a large walled area around the cathedral grounds, containing the cathedral, the bishop's palace, houses for staff, and other buildings. The grounds were covered in grass dotted with ancient gravestones, some of which had been laid flat for safety, and mausoleums erected by wealthy families. Today's memorials tended to be more modest in size.

'I did not know they were police officers at the time but some of the clergy mentioned them the next morning. Perhaps some of my colleagues could assist you?' said the dean.

'So, you never spoke to them?' asked Denison.

'No, I never did,' the dean replied.

'Well, perhaps you can still assist us. Do you own a car, and, if so, what colour is it?' Denison asked.

'Yes, I do. It is a dark blue Ford Mondeo. "Midnight blue", it is called. Quite a nippy little motor.'

'Did you know the young woman who has disappeared, by any chance, Dean?' Denison asked. 'You indicated she lived nearby.'

'Yes, I did, in fact. Well, I met her briefly; must have been about two months ago. November, yes, it was in November. I recognised the name and photograph in the paper. I do hope she turns up safe and well.'

'On what occasion did you meet?' Denison asked.

'Oh, I was participating in some interviews for the position of secretary, with the bishop. She was a candidate. Our current secretary, Mrs Fitzpatrick, is retiring soon. A very able person I thought the young lady was. I was greatly impressed by her interview. I recommended to the bishop that she be put on a shortlist.'

'Thank you. Would you mind calling the others in, sir? Anyone who was here last Tuesday. It would greatly assist us,' said Denison.

The dean lifted an old-style telephone and dialled 0. 'Ah, Miss Smith, would you mind rounding up the staff here at present, who would have been about the cathedral on Tuesday, and ask them to come to my office, please? Just a second.' He covered the mouthpiece. 'Will you need to speak to her, too, Inspector?' Denison nodded. 'Yes, Miss Smith, sorry for keeping you holding. You will have to come yourself as well.'

'Very well, Dean. I'll just set the answering machine for callers.' Miss Smith was a little annoyed: she was just snacking on a tasty salad sandwich and hot sweet coffee. She always brought her own flask of coffee, as she was extremely fussy about the blend. She preferred a special blend of Kenyan beans provided by J.J. Hilditch and Sons of Lichfield. "By Royal Warrant Purveyors of Fine Coffees to H.M. the Queen", their advertisements ran.

The detectives waited patiently. Denison glanced at the clock. The dean glanced at the clock. D.S. Loan glanced at the clock. Presently, there was a knock at the door. 'Come in,' said the dean loudly.

'The staff are here, as am I, Dean,' said Miss Smith as she entered. The others peered in through the doorway.

'These two persons are detectives,' said the dean. 'They wish to ask you all a few questions.' The staff looked mystified and somewhat anxious. 'Would you speak to Miss Smith first, Inspector, as she is required on the switchboard? We do receive numerous telephone calls each day.'

'Yes, that is fine. The rest of you wait outside, please. You too, Dean, if you don't mind,' Denison said.

'Oh yes, but of course. May I get on with some work if I am no longer needed?' said the dean.

'Yes, of course,' replied Denison. 'I shall call you if needed.' Denison did not think the dean would be able to supply much more information.

The dean stood and followed the others out of the room. They sat wherever they could find a seat in the corridor.

'Please take a seat, Miss Smith,' said D. S. Loan. 'What is your first name and where do you live?'

'Jacinta…Jane for short. I have never particularly liked Jacinta. Something I have never forgiven my parents for,' she smiled. 'I live near Burton. I'm wondering why you need to speak to me, Detective?' asked Miss Smith.

'Were you working here last Tuesday, the tenth?' asked Denison.

'Yes, I was. I normally work four days per week on the switchboard, Wednesday to Saturday. Another lady, Mrs Marigold Thornbury-Jones, does Monday and Tuesday, but, as she is ill, I was filling in for her. If we are not too busy, I pursue my hobby of knitting. Children's teddy bears for the hospital. It is closed on Sundays, the switchboard that is, not the hospital.'

'Has this other lady been ill for long?' asked Denison, hoping to move things along.

'Yes. Unfortunately, it is a serious condition. She has been off work since October,' Miss Smith replied.

'Did you see, or speak to, two police officers in the area last Tuesday?'

'Yes, they were asking about some young woman who had disappeared. It is assumed locally that she has been murdered. I told them I never knew her, though she lived nearby it seems. Just outside the cathedral close I believe, according to the papers, but I could not assist them. Will that be all, Officer?' She looked deliberately at her wristwatch.

'Did you, by any chance, see the two officers again in the Edward Street area?' asked Denison, ignoring the hint. He knew she must take that route home.

'Let me think. Yes, I did. I'd almost forgotten. When I was going home at half past five, I noticed them in Edward Street. Well, I'm sure it was them. I live near Burton, you know. Oh, yes, I did mention that, didn't I? They were down by the river talking to each other near the little jetty. They were caught briefly in my headlights as I turned the corner, but it had commenced to snow heavily so I was concentrating on my driving. It can be slippery on that corner, and I had no wish to end up in the river!'

Edward Street ran past the west side of the cathedral close, down a hill to the northern bank of the River Trent, then turned left and followed the river downstream to the city boundary. It then joined a country road that led to Burton-upon-Trent.

'Hmm, well, I think that will be all, for the moment, Miss Smith. You may go. Please send the next person in,' said Denison. D.S. Loan was busy taking notes.

***

At this point, it may be best to add that the missing woman, Miss Clarice Brown, aged twenty-one, was last seen on 26th December going to the Boxing Day sales. She had recently become unemployed when a factory closed and told friends that she was hoping for bargains, as she needed something decent to wear for job interviews.

She was seen by a friend getting into a black car about one p.m. and had not been seen since. The vehicle was a good distance away and the friend could supply few other details, except that a tall, dark-haired man was standing by the car, and he was the driver. The young woman did not seem to be coerced, however, it was widely assumed, by local gossips at least, that she had been abducted and murdered. Extensive searches had been conducted in and around the city especially in the woodland surrounding the castle ruins. The castle, a Royalist stronghold, had been destroyed during the Civil War in the seventeenth century.

***

A grizzled little man was next to enter the dean's office. His trousers were held up by baler twine and his jacket had more holes than a sieve. He had neither washed nor shaved for several days the detectives decided.

'Please take a seat, Mr…?' Denison said, indicating the seat in front of the desk.

'Oh, thankee, don't mind if I do. Me old bones be creaking a bit, and me rheumatis is bothering me somethin' awful,' said the man.

'What is your name, please?' Denison asked again, patiently. He was not interested in the man's ailments.

'Jed Parkinson's the name. I be the odd-job man and occasional gravedigger. Not much call for grave digging since they opened that krematotum thingy two year ago. Lost me a lot of tips that did. Folk were very generous when I dug the graves for their dear departed. Truth be told, I did hang around nearby hoping for tips. A perk of the job, you might say.' He chuckled.

'The crematorium you mean, Mr Parkinson?' said Denison.

'Aye, that be it. Don't be asking me how you spell it,' he laughed.

'Now, were you interviewed by two police officers last Tuesday, and did you know the young lady who has disappeared?' asked Denison.

'Oh yes, I spoke to them, I did. Couldn't tell them anything though. I hadn't seen the young lady for days. I knew the young lady. Very pretty she is or was. I do hope she be all right. Truly kind too. She used to give me a mug of tea and stop for a chat if I was working in the grounds near her little house.'

'And do you know any reason she might have gone away, or if anyone had reason to cause her harm?'

'Oh no, she always seemed so happy and friendly. Can't see anyone wanting to harm her. Not at all. She said she was hoping for a job in the cathedral office. A lovely person she was. I thought of her like the daughter I never had. The missus, she died a year ago yesterday, and I had only boys, six of them, but no girls,' said Mr Parkinson. 'We kept hoping for a girl but were only blessed with boys.' He shook his head slowly, and a tear trickled down his cheek. He rubbed it away with a grubby finger. 'But they be fine lads, all six of them. I have ten grandchildren, I do.' He smiled a toothy smile.

'I'm sorry for your loss. By the way, do you own a car, Mr Parkinson?' Denison asked.

'Nah, never needed one. I have me trusty motorcycle, don't I? That does me; the wife rode pillion, and we took the bus when the boys had to be taken anywhere,' he smiled gently at sweet memories. 'It was some job keeping them seated on the bus, I can tell you.'

'Well, thank you for your help, sir,' said Denison, smiling. He was being unusually patient.

Next in line was the organist. Mrs Lovejoy had been practising for much of that day for an important service coming up: the wedding of the mayor's beloved only daughter Cynthia.

'Mrs Lovejoy how long were you here for on Tuesday?' asked Denison.

'Oh, maybe three or four hours. I do lose track of time when I am playing, sir,' she replied.

'Did you know the young woman who disappeared at Christmas?'

'No, not as far as I can recall. Just a second, I tell a lie! Yes, I did meet her once about a year or more ago. I was playing at the Harvest Thanksgiving, and she said how she enjoyed the music when I was having a cup of tea afterwards.

It was so nice of her. A number of people stayed for tea after the service. We had quite a long chat, we did, but I don't recall ever speaking to her again.'

'Did you see the two detectives at all later that day? Perhaps on your way home?' asked Denison.

'No, I never saw them apart from when they spoke to me. I left soon after that and went home. That was in the afternoon, before dark. I hate driving at night. Not since I nearly hit a policeman in the High Street.' She gave an apologetic grin.

'Well, thank you for your help, Mrs Lovejoy. Please send in the next person,' Denison said.

The next person interviewed was the recently appointed curate, George Matthews, who had just left the "Holy and Undivided Trinity, Anglican Theological College", to give it its full title, in Manchester. He was a young man in his twenties with a lively expression on his handsome face. He was popular with the ladies, especially the unmarried ones. 'Please take a seat,' said Denison and he introduced himself and D.S. Loan.

Matthews sat down. 'How may I assist you, Inspector?' he asked.

'What is your name and your position here in the cathedral? Something clerical judging by your appearance,' said Denison.

'George Matthews, the new curate, to assist the dean. I was appointed last month, just before Christmas, in fact. Chucked in at the deep end, you might say. I'm afraid I sank more than I swam,' he chuckled. Denison ignored the quip. He was getting tired of people wittering on about trivia.

'Were you in this area last Tuesday, Mr Matthews?' Denison asked.

'Erm, yes, I was, for part of the day anyway. I had a dental appointment in the morning, lost a filling. I had to sign on with a new dentist. Got back here about noon, and I was in the office or in the cathedral building for the rest of the day.

'There was a visit at two p.m. from the Mothers' Union from Burton-upon-Trent. About thirty ladies as I recall. Had to show them around, a bit of a history talk, not that I know much yet, so I had to waffle mostly and read from notes. I think some of the ladies found my talk a trifle boring judging by the number of yawns, then tea, cucumber sandwiches and scones in the café. Lots of chatting, as you can imagine.' He smiled. 'Those ladies couldn't half talk. There were three in particular: Edith, Sadie and, erm, yes, Betty—'

Denison interrupted to avoid a long diversion, 'Did you speak to the two detectives who were making enquiries?'

'Yes, but I'm afraid I could not assist them. As I said, I have only come here recently. The unfortunate young woman disappeared about a week or so after I arrived, Inspector. I'm afraid I saw a lot of fresh faces and I don't recall ever meeting her. The last couple of weeks have been terribly busy.'

'Do you own a car, Mr Matthews, and, if so, what colour is it?' asked Denison.

'Yes, I do own one. A little black Fiat, two previous owners. I need it for visits to elderly folk in care homes and hospitals. I get a mileage allowance, fortunately, as there are some twenty premises involved. One is as far away as Wolverhampton.'

'Where do you live, Mr Matthews?' Denison asked.

'Oh, I have a room, I call it the broom cupboard, it is so small, down in Edward Street. At number 46. The landlady is Mrs Love, a widow, and she is a lovely person. Wonderful cook. I am usually only there to sleep and for breakfast and supper, so the size of the room doesn't bother me much. I'm usually so tired I am asleep as soon as my head touches the pillow.'

'Did you see the two detectives down near the river, by any chance?' asked Denison.

'No, I didn't. I got home about six, had a meal, my favourite: eggs, bacon and chips, lots of ketchup, watched some TV and then to bed, early.'

'Hmm, well that will be all for now, Mr Matthews. You may go. Send in the next person, please,' said Denison.

Matthews left and Mrs Mary Thompson, originally from Yorkshire, a cathedral volunteer, walked in and took a seat. She was a large, habitually cheerful character, with rosy cheeks. She introduced herself.

'Mrs Thompson, please take a seat. What is your job in the building?' asked Denison.

After settling herself in a chair, she said, 'Not a job exactly in the normal sense. I'm unpaid you see. I do voluntary work about the place: flower arranging, changing the candles what have burnt too short, bit o' cleaning and dusting, tidying the hymnbooks. That kind o' thing. Terrible mess candles make…wax everywhere, not to mention hundreds of sweet wrappers in those little box thingies on the chairs for holding hymnbooks. Especially at the back of the church where the young 'uns sit.' She tutted. 'I've asked the dean to request non-drip candles when a new supply is ordered.

'I recall a humorous incident once,' she continued without drawing a breath and before Dennison could speak, 'when the sexton was lighting, with a taper on a pole, the four big, tall candles around the altar, must be all of twenty feet tall—the candles that is, not the altar—with the big brass candlesticks. He got three going but the fourth would not light no matter how he tried. There wasn't time to get a stepladder as he had to ring the bell for matins, or were it evensong? Yes, it were evensong. So, he had to go back and snuff out the other three.' She laughed. Dennison frowned. D.S. Loan smiled.

'Were you interviewed by the two detectives last Tuesday?' Denison interjected quickly as he wished to stop more straying from the subject in hand.

'The two what were murdered?' Denison made no reply, only nodded. 'Yes, I met them. Couldn't help them though. I didn't know the young lady what had disappeared. Said in the paper she lived close by, but I never did meet her, I'm sure,' she replied. Her mouth formed a firm line, and she folded her arms as if to finalise things.

'Okay, thank you, Mrs, erm, Thompson. Are there any more staff waiting?'

'Only the bishop himself. Nice man is the bishop. Best 'un we've had since I came to town. Preaches up a storm, he does, an' no mistake. No nodding off to sleep when he's a-preaching, I can tell you. Can't say the same for that new curate though. Poor chap hasn't a clue if you ask me. That's just between you, me and the doorpost.' She winked, stood up, and left.

The bishop entered and sat down. It was not in his nature to have "pulled rank" and gone first as many in his position would have done.

'Ah, Your Grace, I'm sorry to have to take up some of your valuable time but…'

'Think nothing of it, Inspector. And do call me Clarence. No need for titles,' said the bishop, Clarence Clotworthy, a tall, dignified, but humble man of fifty years. What remained of his hair formed a strip of white around the back of his head. His bald pate gleamed like it had been polished.

'Very well, erm, Clarence,' said Denison. 'Were you here last Tuesday, and did you speak to the two detectives?'

'It is a terrible thing. It appears they were murdered,' said the bishop, shaking his head slowly. 'Very sad indeed. Yes, to answer your question, I spoke to them, but I was of little assistance. As far as I can recall, I only met poor Miss Brown once, when she was interviewed about a job as a secretary. There was a large number of applicants. It took three days to meet them all. That was about two weeks before Christmas. I'm afraid I never heard from her again.'

'What makes you think the officers were murdered?' Denison asked, raising an eyebrow.

'Said so in the paper last week they were hit with something: "Struck violently with a blunt instrument," I think it said,' the bishop replied. 'Does not take a Poirot or Holmes to conclude they were murdered. Of course, one cannot believe everything one reads in the papers, can one? "Believe all you read, and you'll eat all you see," as my English teacher used to say back in the day. It's even worse nowadays with "fake news" and conspiracy theories.'

'I suppose so,' said Denison. 'The young woman wanted a job as a secretary. Did she appear agitated in any way? Any indication she had, say, some problems?'

'No, as I recall she seemed perfectly normal. Very relaxed, in fact. She said that she lived nearby so a job here would have been handy. "Just the ticket" was how she put it. Said she was engaged to be married and would I officiate when the time came. Of course, I said I would be delighted. Come to think of it, she never mentioned her fiancé's name. I did ask, but she skirted around it and changed the subject quickly now that I think about it.

'I was about to write to offer her the job, in fact, but I saw her photo in the paper as having disappeared,' the bishop replied.

'Have you got a car, Bishop, and, if so, what colour is it?' D.S. Loan asked.

'Yes, I do. It goes with the job. I have a great deal of travelling to do. It's a black BMW. It's parked in my garage.'

Denison pondered this for a moment. 'I assume you live in the Bishop's Palace,' Denison said.

'Yes, I do. An old Victorian monstrosity. Far too big, in my opinion. You couldn't keep it heated in the winter. Draughts from every door and window. We use only a few of the rooms for that reason, not that my wife and I require so many rooms anyway. In the old days, there would have been a dozen or more servants to clean and keep fires burning, and lots of children, no doubt.'

'Hmm, well, I think that will be all for the moment. We'll be in touch if we need to speak to you again. Thank you,' said Denison.

'Yes, certainly. Good day,' the bishop replied as he left.

***

'Hmm, that's something we didn't know, sir,' said D.S. Mary Loan when they were alone.

'What's that?' enquired Denison, taking his pipe from a pocket and searching for the tobacco pouch. *Drat it, I've forgotten my baccy*, he thought.

'That she was engaged to be wed, sir. No bloke has ever come forward looking for her.'

'Yes, that is strange, very strange indeed,' said Denison, looking puzzled. 'One would imagine he would be banging on our door.' The pipe was replaced in a pocket. *Note to self: bring baccy next time,* Denison thought.

'He could be the bloke in the black car, sir, or she was making it up to impress the bishop,' D.S. Loan suggested. 'Perhaps she thought that being married would give her a better chance of getting the job.'

'Maybe, but I don't see any reason she would make it up really. She would have had to explain why she never got married, were she employed. But it is worth taking note of it.'

Denison continued, 'If her fiancé were the driver then perhaps, they just cleared off together? It would explain why she went willingly.'

'But surely, they would have told their friends, or perhaps seen news bulletins, or read a paper reporting her missing, sir,' said Loan. 'It's been on every news bulletin since Christmas, well, since after Boxing Day.'

'Hmm, it's strange, sure enough. Just our luck everyone seems to drive a dark-coloured car! Well, let's head back to the station, and see what the others think of it, and what they have found out from the Edward Street residents,' Denison said, and they went to their car, Denison's old, rather battered, black Ford Escort. He had difficulty squeezing in behind the wheel. *Must either get a bigger car, or lose weight,* he thought. *A bigger car it is,* he chuckled inwardly and smiled. D.S. Loan wondered why he was smiling but did not comment.

Chapter Two

Enquiries conducted later with close friends of the missing woman concluded that no one had heard of a fiancé. Nobody knew where she was or who the man in the black car had been. Speculation of course was rife. Bunches of flowers began to appear in front of her house and friends held a vigil.

'Right then, troops,' Denison said in the C.I.D. room at police headquarters, his unlit pipe at the side of his mouth, 'have we found out anything more about the missing woman and our two murdered colleagues?' He replaced the pipe in a pocket.

He had called the homicide squad together for a brainstorming session. They were detective constables: Emily Young, Samuel Potter, Sean-Patrick Kelly, and Sandra Johnston with Detective Sergeant Mary Loan. They sat or stood around the incident board, in the main office just outside Denison's, which held photos of the three dead, or presumed dead, and the details of when they were last seen and by whom. It was believed the three deaths were connected. Dennison's office was at one end of this open-plan room separated by wood and glass panelling to give a little privacy when tearing strips off wayward detectives!

D.C. Emily Young said, 'Not much new, sir. The Edward Street residents saw them when they were doing house-to-house enquiries, but apart from them the only other sighting was that woman seeing them by the river. Would we need to interview the residents again, maybe?'

'I see little point in keeping visiting them, Emily,' said Denison. 'At least, not until we have something more substantial to go on.'

'There is speculation among the missing woman's friends, sir,' said D.C. Sam Potter, 'that she has run off with some man. Nobody can identify him though. She was not known to have had a particular beau. In fact, a friend, a Miss Anderson, said,' he looked at his notebook: '"Clarice has not had a boyfriend for about a year that I know of", so it could be that they just don't want to think she may be dead and are just being hopeful. Clinging to hope.'

'Well, she obviously knew the car driver. She was not forced into the car, according to the witness. This gives us something to cling to, but it is not possible to rule out foul play,' Denison said. He tapped a name on the board. 'And she told the bishop she was engaged to be married.'

'Bit difficult tracing a black car with no other details, sir,' said D.C. Potter light-heartedly. The others grinned. Potter was in his twenties, sports-mad and of a habitually cheerful disposition.

'This is not a matter for frivolity, Potter,' Denison growled.

'Er, no, sir, sorry, sir,' Potter muttered. Denison suppressed a smile. His bark was worse than his bite, some of the time.

D.C. Young added, 'Sir, Gwen and John were found on a low mudflat near Blair's Bridge down near Burton-upon-Trent. Somehow they had remained together…' she knuckled away a tear. Taking a deep breath, she continued, 'As we know already, each had received one severe blow to the back of the skull. No other injuries were apparent, according to the pathologist's preliminary report, so could there be more than one suspect?'

D.C. Sean-Patrick Kelly said with an Irish accent, 'Had to be more dan one attacker to be sure, sorr.' His family had left Dublin when he was nine years old, but he had retained his accent.

'So, almost certainly at least two attackers, persons unknown, were involved. I cannot see one person overcoming both of our colleagues,' Denison added. 'Could there be a link with the girl who disappeared? Had they stumbled on something **or** a clue to someone involved?'

'Cannot be ruled out, I suppose, sir,' said D.S. Loan.

'Correct,' said Denison. 'We will continue to operate on the assumption that the three deaths are linked. If the girl is confirmed dead, of course, and not just missing.' Extensive searches of the city and nearby woodland and farms had turned up nothing. 'For her family's sake, I hope she is found, preferably alive.' Everyone agreed.

'Difficult to see a direct connection, sir,' said D.C. Sam Potter. 'If only we had their notebooks. They may have written something down. They were not found on their bodies, so, they may be in the river.'

'What was their last radio report?' Denison asked. 'Can someone read the transcript again, please?'

'At 19:36, John radioed in and reported: "We are just finishing up here in Edward Street, and we have just..." the message ended abruptly, sir,' D.C. Young said as she read from her notes. 'There was a deal of background noise.'

'Sounds like they had found something, sir,' added D.C. Potter, 'then were attacked suddenly.'

'Let's listen to the tape. There may be something in the background noise.

'And, on second thoughts, some of you, Sandra and Sean-Patrick, head for Edward Street.' The two named nodded. 'Interview everyone there again in the houses facing the river, even if they do get stroppy. Remind them that this is a multiple murder enquiry. Ask about any suspicious characters in the area since about New Year, or even Christmas. There is always someone habitually looking out of a window in every street. T.C.S.: Twitching Curtain Syndrome. We must find the killers, and Edward Street holds a clue somehow,' Denison said, banging a fist on the incident board. 'Sam, start a search of the riverbank at Edward Street for those notebooks. We should have done that days ago. My fault, but better late than never. There is a small, muddy space near the jetty on the corner. Bring your wellies.'

'Yes sir, but the attackers could have taken the notebooks,' Potter replied, and he headed to stores to get a pair of wellington boots. Size twelve.

D.I. Denison and D.S. Loan then listened intently to the tape of the last contact from the murdered officers.

'Nothing there that I can hear, sir,' said D.S. Loan. 'Just normal city sounds: cars in the distance; a train is that?'

'Hmm, you're right. It is close to the rail bridge. No, wait! What's that sound? Rewind a bit, Mary.' Loan rewound the tape. 'Yes, d'you hear that *putt, putt*, like a boat engine on the river?' said Denison. 'Slow-moving one by the sounds of it.'

'Yes, it's definitely not a car, sir. Quite a distinct sound…a canal narrowboat perhaps?' suggested D.S. Loan. 'But would there be a canal boat on the river?'

'Sol, you're a boat enthusiast. What do you make of that?' Denison called D.C. Sol Reid, a wiry, dark-haired local man, from his desk at the other end of the room. He was unconnected to the case but was a known boat and fishing enthusiast. Always talking animatedly of "the one that got away".

Sol Reid came over, turned up his hearing aid and listened intently for some seconds. 'Yes, a narrowboat, sir. There are only two guys who have a narrowboat in that area for the winter months: Jimmy Spears and Dave Lappin, friends of mine. Love fishing.'

Reid was deaf in one ear and had problems with the other. He was usually on desk duties because of this. 'I don't mind,' he would say, 'because I can get coffee all day long, and any doughnuts going spare.'

'You're certain?' Denison asked. Denison was pleased with a possible lead.

'Yep, most narrowboat owners stay on the canals, sir. Those two use the moorings on the river this time of year, as there is a lock from the canal to the river from the old days when the canals were more commercial. They live a stone's throw away and it's handy for repairs,' replied Reid. 'Painting and such. Each owner has different painting details on his craft. Immensely proud they are of their boats. Their wives think that they love the boats more than them,' he chuckled.

'Thanks, Sol. Write down their addresses please.' Reid did so and handed the note to Denison. 'Right, Mary we are off for a spot of canal narrow-boating.'

Mary Loan grabbed her coat, gloves, woollen hat and matching scarf. Denison grabbed an overcoat and felt fedora hat. It was cold outside.

Chapter Three

Down by the moorings on the River Trent, about a quarter of a mile upriver from the Edward Street jetty, sure enough, there were two brightly painted narrowboats. The owners had used the winter months to apply fresh paint. The two detectives went over to the nearer one, "The Happy Mermaid", where a man in overalls was busily painting and adding the finishing touches to a small mermaid figurehead on the foredeck.

'Good afternoon, sir,' said Denison. 'Detective Inspector Denison and Detective Sergeant Loan, Castlewood C.I.D. Would you be Mr Spears or Mr Lappin?'

'Dave Lappin's the name. What have I done wrong, Officer?'

'Nothing we know of Mr Lappin. We are just making enquiries,' said Denison.

'Ah, that's okay then,' Lappin chuckled. He set his paintbrush down and wiped his hands on a cloth. 'I won't shake hands,' he chuckled.

'A football fan I see,' said Denison, indicating Lappin's black and yellow scarf and matching woollen cap pulled down over his ears. Football emblems could also be seen in the cabin windows.

'Oh, yes, Burton Albion fan all my life, me. Come on you Brewers!' Lappin chanted, punching a fist in the air.

'Follow them a bit myself,' said Denison. 'Don't get much time to attend matches though, to be honest.'

'Did you see the new signing from Leeds City score that hat trick last Saturday? Luke Parker he's called, a local lad from Rugeley. Just turned nineteen.'

'Yes, and he is in line for an England cap before long I would think,' said Denison.

'Wow, marvellous he was. Scored an equaliser with ten minutes to go, and the winner thirty seconds from the whistle! The club's most expensive signing ever. Money well spent was that,' Lappin enthused. 'Not that Burton buy many players; we don't have wads of cash like some clubs.'

'I only saw the highlights on the telly, unfortunately,' said Denison, 'but he was great. Only nineteen, too. He reminds me of George Best.'

D.S. Loan rolled her eyes skyward with a wry smile. *You boys and your football,* she thought.

'"The Brewers" is a good nickname being as Burton is famous for brewing beer. Apparently, the water supply is ideal for the best beer,' Denison continued. 'Did you know Mary, Queen of Scots, got her supplies from Burton?'

'Her what got her head chopped off? No, I never knew that. Wow! That's interesting,' said Lappin.

'When she was imprisoned by Elizabeth I in Chartley Manor, she had a lot of maids and servants and such who needed liquid refreshment,' Denison grinned. 'A Burton brewer was paid to smuggle secret messages from Mary to her supporters. Unfortunately for her, the brewer was also paid to pass the messages to Queen Elizabeth's agent first. I forget his name. The rest is history as they say.' He chuckled.

Denison continued, 'Getting back to business, last Tuesday evening, the tenth, were you by any chance on your boat near the Edward Street jetty?'

'Aye, I was sure enough. I had overhauled the motor and went down the river a few miles and back, to see how she was running,' replied Lappin.

'And you passed that area at the Edward Street jetty?'

'Yes, and I turned back about a mile or so after that and returned here. The motor was running like clockwork. Really sweet. Saved myself a lot of cash I did by doing it myself. Mechanics cost a bomb.'

'Did you happen to notice two people on the riverbank?' asked Denison.

'Would that be the two cops that were bumped off, erm, sorry, murdered?' asked Lappin. 'I heard something about them being in Edward Street.'

'Did you see anyone, Mr Lappin?' Denison repeated himself getting a little annoyed.

'Aye, as you mention it, I did see two people. The boat goes slowly so I was looking around to pass the time. It was too dark to see who, for they were facing away from the streetlights, and I was in the middle of the river, but they were standing talking, it looked like. One had a phone to his ear it looked like. I say "his" because I assume it was a bloke, as he was the taller of the two. Really tall he was.'

'And were they still there when you returned?' D.S. Loan asked.

'Nope, they were gone. Not a sign of them, Sergeant. Oh, but I did notice a car driving off up the hill towards the cathedral in a hurry,' said Lappin. 'I say "driving off" but going like the clappers it was. Screeching tyres. Car thieves, I thought to myself, I did. Meant to call the cops but it went out of my head. I'd forget my head if it weren't screwed on,' he chuckled. The officers did not.

'Any chance you could describe it?' asked Denison hopefully.

'Nah, just a car, dark colour possibly, no lights on till it was well up the street, and some of the streetlights were out, as usual. Council is useless.'

'Any idea of the time this occurred?' asked Denison.

'Hmm, now you're asking. Seven-thirty? No, near seven forty-five as the cathedral clock struck the three quarters just afterwards. I remember checking my watch. It's forever going slow. Must get a new one.

'I tied up here before I went home, arriving about eight because "Coronation Street" was just finishing. The wife loves it. I think it was an extra episode 'cause it is not usually on on a Tuesday,' Lappin replied.

Denison sighed inwardly. *Why do I get them all?* he thought. 'Thank you, Mr Lappin, you've been extremely helpful. Do you happen to know if Mr Spears is at home?'

'Jimmy?'

Denison nodded. *How many Mr Spears do you know?* he thought.

'Yes, he should be, but he wasn't about that Tuesday night if that is what you wish to know. He and his missus went to the cinema, Cineworld, in Burton if I remember correctly. Some Ryan Reynolds' film Mrs S wanted to see. They were right shocked when they heard what happened. Cissy, Mrs Spears that is, said: "Those poor people getting done in and us laughing our heads off in the pictures." Yes, terribly upset she was,' Lappin added.

'We'll have a chat anyway. Thanks again, sir,' said Denison.

'No problem. Hope you catch the killers,' Lappin said. He resumed his painting.

'We will,' replied Denison. 'We certainly will.'

Nothing more was uncovered when they spoke to Mr and Mrs Spears. They confirmed that they had been watching a comedy in the cinema and were not home until late. They had stopped for fish and chips, and tea, bread and butter in a café, The Royal, on the way home. 'A special treat as it was Jimmy's birthday. Sixty he was,' Mrs Spears had said.

Chapter Four

'Excuse me, Officer,' said a young woman as she approached the enquiry desk in the Castlewood city centre police headquarters. She was accompanied by a tall young man who looked embarrassed as he shuffled from foot to foot, his hands in his pockets.

'Yes, Miss, what can I do for you?' asked the sergeant on duty. The young woman raised her left hand "casually" to tidy a stray hair, displaying a gleaming wedding ring. 'I beg your pardon, Madam,' said the sergeant, 'how can I assist you?' He smiled at the obvious hint.

'I hope you can, Sergeant. It is a rather strange, unique even, problem. You see it appears that I am missing!' She blushed with embarrassment.

'I don't understand, Madam, you appear to be here…in one piece…in the flesh, so to speak,' replied the sergeant. He thought, *we've got a right one here. A bit like a Basil Fawlty sketch.*

'My name is, was, Clarice Brown. I am now Mrs Sanders, Mrs Richard Sanders.' She grinned at her spouse, the aforementioned Richard Sanders. He blushed.

'Oh…the young woman who disappeared on Boxing Day?' exclaimed the sergeant. 'Only, you didn't. Obviously!'

'Yes, exactly, Sergeant, except I didn't, at least not in a bad way. You see my fiancé, Richard here,' she blushed, 'and I eloped to bonny Scotland, got married at Gretna Green just across the border and went on honeymoon to a remote Scottish island. Very remote. About as remote as you can get and only a tiny dot on the map. We thought it was a speck of dirt on the map at first. It doesn't have a proper name. Just a Gaelic name *Eilean Beag,* if I remember correctly, meaning "A Little Island" we were told. Isn't that right, Richard?'

Richard replied, 'Erm, think so, Dearest. Not good at languages, me.' His hands sank deeper into his pockets.

'Anyway, we stayed in a little thatched croft, outside toilet, no plumbing except for one cold tap from a tank of rainwater, and with no TV, no radio, nor phones, so we only discovered the news of my "disappearance" when we returned to the mainland early this morning.'

'Never again,' Richard muttered.

'You had better speak to the detectives in charge, Madam. There has been quite a hunt for you,' the sergeant looked stern. 'Take a seat for a minute, please.' The two sat down and clasped hands, gazing lovingly into each other's eyes. The sergeant lifted a receiver and telephoned the C.I.D. room.

'Do you remember the missing young woman?' he asked.

'Of course, I do, Sergeant. What are you wittering about, man?' said the detective.

'Well, she isn't. Missing that is. She's here at the desk, large as life. And married.' He smiled.

'I'll be right out.' The detective shook his head. *If this is some kind of joke…*

39

Seconds later, D.I. Denison opened a door and enquired, 'Miss Brown, as was?'

'Erm, yes, Officer. I am dreadfully sorry for causing such a fuss. It appears that you all thought I had been murdered!'

'Well, thankfully, you were not,' Denison replied. 'This, may I assume, is your husband?' Denison looked at Richard. *Hmm, a skinny looking critter,* he thought. *Hope she is a good cook, for his sake.*

'Yes, sir, I am that lucky man, Richard Sanders by name,' said Richard, shaking hands, and he grinned like the Cheshire Cat.

'Please come this way,' said Denison and they went down a corridor to a vacant interview room. D.S. Loan was waiting there.

'Right then, I am Detective Inspector Denison, and my colleague is Detective Sergeant Mary Loan. Do take a seat, Mr and Mrs Sanders.' Loan looked puzzled until Denison explained the change of name.

'Congratulations,' Loan said and smiled. The pair grinned.

Denison said, 'So, you have been out of touch since December, Mrs Sanders. In exile, so to speak.'

'Yes, as I told the nice man at the desk we were on a remote island. Well, very remote. We did not appreciate how remote when we booked it. Never again! It was like being back in the seventeenth century. I would swear we saw a ghost one night.' She shuddered and Richard nodded. 'But it might have been a sheep. Then it blew up a storm something awful and we could not get back to the mainland for days. The boatman and owner of the cottage, Frazier MacDougal, of the Argyle MacDougals as he kept saying, had not ventured out.

Inconvenient but sensible really. "Mare than ma life's worth," he said.' She tried to imitate his accent.

'I suppose it was silly not telling my friends what I was doing, but my previous boyfriend turned out to be…I'll not use the words. Long story short: he never turned up for our wedding! There I was all dressed up, ready to walk up the aisle and no groom! The rat had run off to Canada with a tart and part of my savings as I discovered later. I got loads of banter from friends. I know they did not mean any harm, but I decided this time to keep it all secret. It seemed a clever idea at the time but a mistake as it turns out,' said Clarice.

'You have caused a lot of bother and worry to a lot of people, young lady,' Denison sounded cross. D.S. Loan was stifling a laugh.

'Erm, well, yes, and I am terribly sorry, Inspector.' Clarice looked mortified.

'Well, I suppose we can call off the murder hunt,' said Denison with the hint of a smile. 'I shall inform the press that you are alive and well. You can expect a horde of reporters at your door, I'm afraid, wanting your story.' Clarice grimaced. 'Be sure to charge them plenty,' he laughed. 'Should you ever decide to get married again please tell someone and save us a lot of bother,' he laughed again. D.S. Loan laughed too.

'I certainly have no intention of ever having another wedding, Inspector. My darling hubby, Richard, is stuck with me for life,' she chuckled. The couple smiled at each other adoringly.

'Thank you for being so understanding,' Richard said.

'No problem. "All's well that ends well," as someone once wrote,' said Denison.

D.S. Loan raised a surprised eyebrow at Denison quoting literature but wisely refrained from comment.

Loan said, 'I expect you two are hungry. I'll take you up to our canteen. Does hot homemade soup and fresh bread rolls sound good?'

'Sounds delicious,' the two chorused.

'I might join you,' Denison joked. It had been a long time since breakfast.

Chapter Five

'Well, that's one case solved anyway, sir. It certainly means our two colleagues did not uncover anything about her supposed death,' said D.C. Sam Potter as the team gathered around later. 'But what on earth did they come across that caused them to be murdered?'

'Yes, they must have stumbled on someone or something. A terrorist cell maybe,' suggested D.C. Sandra Johnston.

'There is only one way to find out: catch the perpetrators,' said Denison with a grim expression. He had to resist the urge to light his pipe. His mind was clearer when he was smoking his pipe he believed. *Worked for Sherlock Holmes,* he often thought.

D.C. Kelly said in his Irish accent, 'No one saw or heard anyt'ing dat evening in Edward Street, sorr. All were watching some comedy show on da TV. Immensely popular so it seems, to be sure. Da man in number 63 seems to have been the last resident to speak to them. He t'inks it was 'bout seven-t'irty. But dat is only a guess. Da curate, what's-his-name, Matthews, has a room dere, at number 46, but he wasn't in, but we have already spoken to him anyway.'

'No trace of their notebooks either, sir. I searched until dark. It was a longshot anyway,' Potter added. 'Got mud to the eyes anyway for my trouble.'

'We need to visit that curate again,' said Denison.

There was a tap on the door which was ajar. 'Come in!' Denison said.

The pathologist, Samantha Nixon, came in and said, 'Sorry for barging in, Inspector, but I thought you would want this immediately.' She handed a report to Denison.

'Ah! This could be the lead we needed,' he exclaimed when he had read it. 'Hit by an object or objects with a narrow shaft and a thick club-like top, possibly of wood,' he quoted.

'They both had water in the lungs, so I'm afraid they were alive when thrown in the river,' Nixon added. The detectives gasped at what this implied.

'Golf clubs?' suggested D.C. Potter, who was also a keen golfer.

'Sounds like it could be,' said Samantha Nixon. 'They would certainly be a possibility.'

'Thank you, Samantha, this is a great help,' said Denison.

'No problem, sir. Goodnight, everyone,' Samantha Nixon said and left. They all said goodnight in unison.

'Okay, we'll call it a day, gang. Back here tomorrow morning at nine, sharp,' said Denison. They all said goodnight again and left.

***

Sunday, January 15th

'Thank you all for giving up your day of rest, ladies and gents,' said Denison the next morning.

'Be worth it to catch the killers, sir. Gwen and John were two of the best,' said D.S. Loan. All murmured agreement.

'Right, anyone got any ideas how to proceed? I've been pondering it all night, hence the bags under my eyes,' Denison said after a moment's pause.

Not a few thought, *You always have bags under your eyes.*

There was silence. No one spoke. Some shook their heads in despair.

'That boat owner said he saw them by the river. It coincides with the last message, but they were gone when he returned at about seven forty-five,' said D.S. Loan.

'He heard the clock chime a quarter to eight, so we can take that as not long after the time of death for he saw a car speeding off up the hill. A dark-coloured car. But as it was night and about four streetlights were out, it could have been almost any colour,' added D.C. Young. 'So, he must have just missed the killings by minutes or even seconds.'

'By minutes given the time of their last message,' said Denison. 'We have to remember Mr Lappin was out on the river and, I'm sure, not really paying close attention. It is just because the narrowboat is slow-moving that he noticed anything.'

'We can assume, sorr, dat in the time it took him to go down da river and back, our colleagues were attacked and dumped in da river. Must have been quick, so,' said D.C. Kelly.

'In that case, I would think it is certain there was more than one assailant, and they were nearby. That is possibly living in that street,' said D.C. Potter.

'Two or more. But who and why?' said D.C. Emily Young. Silence again. 'What else could they have stumbled on in that street?' she added. 'The residents are mainly elderly folk and unlikely to indulge in hitting people with golf clubs.'

'Right,' Denison said, 'I want the riverbed searched for about one hundred yards each direction. Chances are the killers chucked the clubs or whatever into the river. We'll assume they are golf clubs for the moment. Mary, phone the "dive and search" guys in Newcastle, please.'

'Sure, sir,' D.S. Lone replied, lifted a phone and consulted a list of numbers.

The squad spent the rest of the day, while the divers were at work, going through recent cases which D.S. Travis and D.C. Savage had been involved in. None seemed to have been involving potential murderers: only burglaries and car thefts. It was disheartening.

That evening, at about half past five, Denison said, 'All right, gang, we may as well wrap it up for today. We're not getting anywhere fast and the divers will have quit now that it's dark.

'Sam, in the morning, contact our local informants. See if they have heard of anything which may be useful. Offer a reward for anything which brings a conviction.'

'Sure thing, Boss,' D.C. Potter replied. 'Billy "the Beak" Bowler, he has a long nose, is a likely candidate who springs to mind. If there is info out there, he will know it. I'll try to meet him this evening.'

'Okay, see you all in the morning. Sleep well,' Denison said, and he turned off the light as they exited.

***

Monday, January 16th

The team gathered on the following morning. No one was in a good mood, not even Potter, who could normally have raised a laugh in a Trappist monastery.

'Good morning. Are we all here? Good,' said Denison trying to be upbeat as he breezed into his office. The team were sitting or standing around his desk. 'As you are aware, it is a week since our colleagues were murdered and we have not a useful clue to go on. Is there any word from Billy the Beak, Sam?'

'I have arranged to meet with him this morning, sir,' D.C. Potter replied. 'He wants to be treated to breakfast.' The others laughed.

'Good,' Denison said. 'That's a start anyway. Sam, Emily and…let's see…yes, Sean-Patrick, for some muscle…' he joked, the rest smiled. Sean-Patrick was a big guy: every spare minute was spent in the gym. 'You can try to feel a few collars if Billy gives some names.'

'Yes, sir,' the three replied enthusiastically as one.

Potter and the other two got their heads together to plan a strategy.

'First, we need to get hold of Billy. Wring out of him everything he knows,' said Potter. 'He was in his local pub "Old Bull and Bush" last night when I phoned him, and he was reluctant to talk. "Too many ears and wagging tongues", he said.'

'Can hardly blame him for being cautious. Those gangs play for keeps. There would have been another body floating in the Trent,' said D.C. Emily Young.

'Okay, we will head for Billy's digs. He said he stays in a boarding house in Mary Street,' Potter said.

Billy "the Beak" Bowler was still snoring when his landlady let the three detectives into his room. They could get no response to their knocking except a growled 'Clear off,' from Billy.

''Ere, what's your game?' he shouted, rubbing sleep from his eyes. 'Oh, it's you lot,' Billy said. 'Can't a hard-working bloke get a few hours' kip without the "Old Bill" bursting into his private accommodation?'

'Are you kidding, Billy? You never did a hard day's work in your entire life...nothing honest anyway,' Potter replied.

Bowler grunted. 'That's as may be, but you have no right to come in here uninvited! You got a warrant? At least give me a minute to get me kit on, ladies present, an' I'm not decent. I'm in me boxers.' He was holding the duvet up to his chin. Mrs Scruggs, the landlady, was still in the doorway and Billy nodded towards her and D.C. Young.

'Gone all shy have you, Billy? Tell you what, we'll wait for you on the landing for five minutes. We are on the third floor so I don't think you will be jumping out of the window,' D.C. Potter said with a chuckle. 'Thank you, Mrs Scruggs, that will be all.'

Mrs Scruggs reluctantly went downstairs muttering to herself.

Minutes later, the toilet flushed and Billy, full dressed, appeared. The three detectives and he adjourned to a nearby eatery which went by the grandiose name "The Gastronomic Delight Café". It did not live up to the name. But Billy was glad to tuck into a full English and more: four sausages, two fried eggs, bacon (two thick slices), black pudding, tomatoes, mushrooms (double portion), beans and fried bread. And toast. He was making the most of his free meal. *Where does he put it all?* D.C. Emily Young wondered. The three detectives had coffee and toast.

'Ah, that hit the spot,' he declared as he mopped up the remaining egg yolk with a last piece of toast and swigged down the last of his third mug of tea. He sat back, patting his stomach with one hand and licking the fingers of the other. 'Most satisfying, I must say. Would your lot care to provide that every morning?' he asked hopefully. The police officers ignored him.

'Let's get down to business, Billy. Where are the gang members we spoke of hiding out?' D.C. Potter asked.

'You never heard nothing from me, right?' Billy looked each one in the eye, in turn.

'We don't even know you, Mr Whatever-your-name-is,' D.C. Young said.

'This conversation never happened,' said D.C. Potter.

Billy mentioned a couple of guys from Manchester who were hiding out in Castlewood. Another gang was after blood, due to drug money or something, so they had made themselves scarce. He did not know the exact addresses, but a lowlife called Jacob "Jake" Harvey was possibly somewhere around Edward Street, and his accomplice,

Sidney "Slasher" Malone, in the city centre near Handel Street.

'Hmm, Edward Street,' Potter said to his colleagues as they got into their car. 'Could that be who Gwen and John discovered that night?'

'Sounds very like it but I don't remember any young guys living in dat street,' said D.C. Kelly.

Chapter Six

'I have just received some unwelcome news, troops,' said Denison the next day about eleven a.m. The assembled detectives listened intently. 'Billy Bowler, our informant, was found murdered this morning. About an hour ago.' Everyone gasped. 'At least, they found what was left of him.

'Maisie Scruggs, his landlady, had been out shopping and when she returned, she went up to his room to ask if he wanted breakfast. Billy was not an early riser. When she got no reply, she opened his door with her key only to find the room splattered with blood. Billy's remains were almost unidentifiable: his face and torso had been mutilated; I won't go into detail; I will just leave it to your imagination. They carved their gang's initials on his chest: BCW for the "Big City Warriors" we assume. The pathologist thinks he was still alive when they did it.

'Mrs Scruggs told uniform what she could before being sedated. The doctor says she could be traumatised for weeks. The poor woman may never fully recover and will be taken to a nursing home for a while. Her other guests will be moving out. Quite understandable really. Fortunately, for them, I suppose, they had all been out at work at the time of the attack.'

'It was only yesterday when we spoke to him, sir,' said Sam Potter, his face pale. 'He was right to be scared as it turns out.' The others nodded in agreement. 'It would seem that somehow the gang found out that he had been speaking to us.'

'He gave us two names, sorr,' said D.C. Kelly. 'Sidney Malone and Jacob Harvey. Both have form for violence: Malone is nicknamed "Slasher" so top o' the list for Billy's death, and Jacob Harvey, known as Jake, is a younger sidekick. Vicious little brute too. I assume they are the "Big City Warriors". Billy didn't know exactly where they were hiding out, but he t'ought Jake Harvey was somewhere around Edward Street and Sid Malone in the city centre in the Handel Street area. 'Tis a rough neighbourhood to be sure.'

Denison said, 'Manchester have confirmed those two lowlifes and one or two cronies call themselves the Big City Warriors. So at least now we know who to look for. Nice of them to leave a clue. There used to be about four more in the gang, but they have been killed by other gangs or are locked up.'

***

Sid Malone was a thin wiry man, aged thirty-three, clean-shaven normally, with little hair left on his head. His face was shrewd and usually had an unnerving sly "smile" on the lips.

Jake Harvey was aged twenty-one, had dark, wavy hair and of a handsome appearance, which concealed his brutal character.

'Hmm, that's interesting. Edward Street is cropping up regularly,' Denison commented. 'I don't recall a young man living there though, except for the curate from St John's. But it is just possible our colleagues recognised someone, and they were about to call backup when they were attacked. We need to find out if anyone has left there in a hurry.

'Right, I want every available body out searching Edward Street's houses from attic to cellar, if they have any. I'll get search warrants issued ASAP.'

'Dere'll not be any cellars, sorr. Dey are too close to da river, sorr, I'm t'inking,' Kelly commented.

'It's just a saying, Sean-Patrick,' Denison grinned. Kelly went red, feeling silly. He tended to take everything literally.

Later that day, the street in question was cordoned off by the police. No one was allowed in or out. A systematic search was conducted on every property and outbuilding. All the residents, who were mainly retired folk who had lived there most of their lives, were interviewed again. They had heard of the gruesome murder of Billy Bowler but knew of no likely candidate in the street.

D.C. Potter later commented, 'There were only two young men living in the street: George Matthews, the curate we know about, who obviously is still living here; and Olly Farringdon, a war veteran, who has no legs. Both are beyond suspicion, I would think.'

'Might be jumping to a conclusion, but I cannot see either of them hitting people over the head,' commented Denison. 'Still, must keep an open mind.'

Just then a constable came out of number 46 carrying an old red and white golf bag. He had wrapped a handkerchief around the handle. 'Inspector, I found this under the stairs in this house. The lady said it belonged to her late husband but had not been used since he died. The driver and another club are missing if I am not mistaken. There are two of those little covers off the clubs left behind. I never touched them in case they have prints. Pretty top-of-the-range piece of kit, I would guess.'

'Very true, Constable. Very expensive set indeed, by the looks of it,' said Denison. He thought golf rather too energetic.

'Number 46? Isn't that where the curate lives?' asked D.C. Potter.

The constable replied, 'It is, but the owner says he is away somewhere today, and he never plays golf.'

'We must have a word in his shell-like, tomorrow,' Denison replied. 'Perhaps he had a visitor.'

Officers tried to reassure those residents who were now nervous for their own safety as word spread. A police car would be making regular patrols in the area until the killers were apprehended.

Chapter Seven

Wednesday, January 18th

It was a bitterly cold day. A "Beast from the East" weather front had descended on eastern England. Penguins would have felt at home as snow fell constantly and was piling into drifts against any obstacle. The city hospital's Accident and Emergency Department was full of broken bones from falls and car accidents. One vehicle had skidded two hundred yards down a hill, bouncing off three vehicles before hitting a wall and coming to a crunching stop.

Denison called the crew together. 'We are going to have to fight our way through the snow, troops. There is nothing else for it. The top brass won't be happy if we are not making progress.' The detectives had come well provided for with warm clothing.

'I'll get that pair's photos off records and get them copied,' said D.C. Potter and he tapped at the computer keyboard.

Just then, D.C. Emily Young entered noisily, waving a printout from a computer. 'Sorry to barge in, sir, but this has just arrived by email from Manchester C.I.D.'

'What does it say?' Denison asked and he took the sheet and read it. His face turned pale.

'What does it say, sorr?' asked Kelly.

Denison read aloud, '"Tuesday, 17th. January. A body has been found in a freezer in a block of flats used by students. The body has been identified,"' he paused, trying to take in the words, '"as that of George Matthews, a student at the Theological College."' Everyone stood open-mouthed.

'But…but that's the curate's name!' D.C. Johnston exclaimed.

D.C. Potter, who had been to a printer to get the mugshots copied, said, 'Sir, look at these mugshots of the two crims. One looks exactly like the cathedral cur…' Before he could finish, Denison handed him the printout of the email.

'Wow! The curate!' Potter exclaimed. 'Like twins, aren't they?'

'Exactly. Grab your hat and coat, D.S. Loan, we need to have a word with that guy. Obviously, he is not whom he claims to be,' Denison exclaimed as he popped a hat on his head and grabbed a coat, scarf and umbrella. *Should have brought gloves,* he thought.

'I'll just nip to the ladies, first, sir, if I may?' D.S. Loan said.

'Okay, needs must,' Denison replied with a smile.

Arriving at the cathedral minutes later, the doors were closed. No visitors were expected that day as all booked visits had rung in to cancel due to the weather. Denison banged loudly on the door to the offices. There were lights on, so somebody was in.

'Ah, it's you, Inspector and Sergeant,' the dean, who had been passing by the door, said in surprise as he opened it. 'Do come in. Rather inclement weather to be out and about.' He shivered as a mini snow blizzard blew in around him.

The detectives were already pushing past him. 'Where is the curate, Matthews?' Denison demanded brusquely.

'Why, he will be in the office down the corridor, the one with the brown door, at some paperwork. At least he was earlier. I was speaking to…'

Denison was already striding towards the office indicated. D.S. Loan followed him.

He threw open the door and glanced around the room as heads turned in his direction.

'Where's George Matthews?' he demanded.

'He was here a few minutes ago,' said a small grey-haired lady, who looked up from her typewriter, gold-rimmed spectacles on a chain perched on her nose. 'He seems to have slipped out. He received a text on his telephone a few minutes ago and left abruptly. Never finished his coffee.' She indicated a mug sitting on a table.

'How did he know?' Denison said quietly to D.S. Loan. He was more than puzzled.

'He obviously got a tipoff, sir. That means there is a leak in Manchester Met's C.I.D.'

'Or a leak here in our C.I.D,' suggested Denison. He turned to the dean who was looking bewildered.

'I am afraid your curate was an imposter, sir. He is quite possibly responsible for four murders that we know of, including the real George Matthews. We think he is, in fact, Jake Harvey, a known criminal.' Everyone in the office gasped and looked at each other. The dean went pale.

'You mean that George, or Jake Harvey, or whatever he is called, is the killer of the two detectives found by the river and the real George Matthews? Oh dear, oh dear, that is horrible.'

The dean, stunned-looking, sat down on the nearest chair as his legs went weak.

'Oh, good heavens! He could have murdered us all!' screamed the typist, putting her hands to the sides of her face. Another lady fainted.

'I did wonder how he got the job as curate as he knew little of the Scriptures. I put it down to new-boy nerves, and I was contemplating speaking to the bishop about him, and now we know why,' said the dean. His face was as white as a sheet. Denison feared that the dean was going to be sick and asked one of the staff to help him.

'Well, you may look for a replacement, Dean. The real Mr Matthews was found murdered and hidden in a freezer. They are almost identical, like twins,' said Denison and he and D.S. Loan left. The room erupted in chatter, everyone speaking at once.

As they approached their car, the sirens of fire engines could be heard. A plume of smoke arose from the direction of the river. Thankfully, the snow had ceased.

'I have a gut feeling that might be to do with Harvey,' said Denison. 'Jump in.' He drove as quickly as possible, given the road conditions, down towards the river. A fire officer stepped out into the road, which had been freshly gritted and stopped them about one hundred yards from the fire. Then a uniformed constable approached the car.

'I'm afraid, this is as close as you can go, sir. Oh. It's yourself, Inspector Denison,' he said. 'A car is on fire, arson it looks like. The firefighters say the flames have reached the fuel tank.'

'Thank you, Constable. I have a good idea who did it. We were just on our way to try to nab him,' Denison said.

'Afraid he is long gone, sir. A witness said the curate, of all people, pushed her to the ground and threw a match into the car. It had been doused in petrol or something flammable. Then the man was met by a bloke in a dark red car, no make or full number, unfortunately. She said its registration plate began with *AB*. That's all she could see because it was covered in muddy slush.'

'Very well. Radio it in, Constable. You're Constable McFlynn, aren't you?' said Denison.

'Yes, sir, Andy McFlynn. I'll get them to search registration records for a red motor with the reg. number beginning with the letters *AB*.'

'Okay, but I would wager it is a fake plate. We'll be on our way. Thank you, Andy,' said Denison, and he turned the car and drove off.

Chapter Eight

Back at police headquarters, Denison consulted with his superior about the apparent leak.

'Sir, it has become evident that the criminal, Jake Harvey, we were after has been tipped off by someone either here, or in Manchester.'

'Hmm, whoever warned him will pay dearly when caught, I can promise you that,' said the Chief Superintendent of Castlewood, John Harris. He felt betrayed to think that someone in his station could be an accomplice of criminals.

'It could still be in Manchester, the leak, sir,' D.I. Denison tried to smooth things. He, too, was anxious about an accomplice.

Harris replied, 'Yes, but they knew yesterday that the body of the real George Matthews had been found, so why was the curate, fake curate, only texted a few minutes before you arrived? No, the culprit must be here. It stinks! If the media get a whiff of this...

'We need to winkle out this mole, Denison, and quickly!' said Harris banging his fist on a desk.

'Yes, sir, I intend to do just that,' said Denison.

Dennison and D.S. Loan made a list of all the officers in Castlewood police station who may have known about the fake curate prior to their visit to the cathedral.

'Well, sir,' said D.S. Loan, 'there is you and me, Emily, Sammy, Sean-Pat, and Sandra.'

'Plus, anyone who might have seen the notice Emily brought in. Get her in here, please,' said Denison. Mary Loan went into the main office and called D.C. Emily Young.

'What's up, sir?' Young asked, wondering what was going on.

'When the notice about the dead student arrived from Manchester in the emails, apart from us in this team, who all may have seen it?' asked Denison.

'Only me, sir. I got a phone call from Manchester saying to check for an urgent e-mail. There was no one else nearby, except...who was it? Yes, Samantha Nixon from pathology who was passing through. She just said "Hi". All our lot were with you in here. I went to the printer and got a printout, then signed off the computer before I came to you,' D.C. Young said. 'No one saw the printout or the screen, I'm certain.'

'All right, Emily, you may go,' said Denison. D.C. Young left the room looking worried.

'Hmm, it looks like we have an informer in our midst, sir, in the building,' said D.S. Loan, shaking her head slowly. 'Could it be Samantha Nixon?'

'Much as I hate to admit it, yes. I know it is not me, and I'm certain it isn't you. We have worked together for too long not to trust you,' he smiled. D.S. Loan nodded her appreciation.

Denison continued, 'I want you to check discretely the troops' files. Has anyone any connection with Manchester, specifically a connection with Malone and Harvey? A previous arrest made or something, anything. I cannot think of anyone offhand.'

Later, D.S. Loan had produced nothing. 'There is no obvious connection between Manchester and the detectives here in Castlewood. None has ever served in the Manchester Met. or been involved in an arrest of those two.'

'Right, start a house-to-house search in the Handel Street area. Malone may still be around. The mole will slip up sometime, and when they do, may the Lord have mercy on their soul, for I certainly won't,' Denison declared to Loan.

She nodded. 'Yes, sir, I'll get it organised right away.'

Several streets were cordoned off by the police in that area of the city, and every resident was questioned. One person recalled a man who looked like Malone's photo living in a one-bed flat at 15, Purcell Street. Malone, however, was now nowhere to be seen when the house was visited. It was confirmed that he drove a dark red car, and the flat had been hurriedly vacated. The landlord was owed two weeks' rent, and he was not pleased.

'Thanks to you coppers I'm out, erm, four weeks' rent from that guy. Who's going to compensate me?' The police ignored him.

'Looks like he was warned that we had a possible address, sir. If we only knew who told him,' said D.S. Loan to Denison.

The search for the two suspects was widened to cover the neighbouring counties and Manchester. Denison thought that the two could hide out among their underworld cronies.

Chapter Nine

'If we get a lead on where those two are,' suggested Denison to Loan as he tapped a finger on their photos on the incident board, 'could we let the team know and find out which one, if any, sends a warning text or call to them?'

'Hmm, it might work, sir. Could be worth a try as it might smoke out the culprit,' D.S. Loan replied. 'But just suppose none of them is guilty, it will destroy the team's morale.'

'No one likes not to be trusted,' said Denison. 'We will just have to take a chance on that. Ensure only a few in Manchester and us two know about it. I could hold a briefing just to bring them up to date. Something like, "There has been a development. Manchester C.I.D. are preparing to nab Harvey and Malone at such and such address."'

Denison continued, 'We'll give it a go. We'll have to hope a lead comes soon. I will contact Manchester's Chief Superintendent to get his agreement and to make certain as few as possible know the details. He can set a watch on the place the criminals are staying, if they are hiding out together then we tell the team, grab their phones when the pair scarper and see who texted. Right, I'm off home.'

'Me too, I'm completely shattered, sir. A good night's sleep is what's needed,' said D.S. Loan.

Denison grabbed his hat and coat and bustled out to his car. He had to scrape a covering of ice from the windscreen.

**

Saturday, January 21ˢᵗ

Every informer in the surrounding towns in six counties and in Manchester had been contacted. A large reward was offered for information leading to a conviction, but most were too fearful to get involved because of the reputation of the two men concerned. They had all heard of the fate of Billy "the Beak" Butler.

The Chief Superintendent of Manchester Metropolitan Police had almost given up hope for the plan, when an informer, using a code name, "Rudolf", indicated that Malone, and possibly Harvey, was holed up at a certain address in Eccles, an area of Manchester.

Only three high-ranking officers in Manchester knew of this as Rudolf had contacted the Chief Superintendent directly and he phoned D.I. Denison personally.

'D.I. Denison here,' he answered when his phone rang.

'Ah, Denison, Chief Super. Pallister, Manchester, here. We have a possible address for the two you are looking for. Well, it seems pretty certain as my informer is dependable.'

'That's great news, sir,' Denison replied. Pallister then relayed the information.

'I have a reliable man watching the house. He is to report to me, and only me, and then to follow or have a car follow the occupants should they leave. He has my mobile phone number and more men on standby to follow them. They have not been informed of who the occupants are, only to look for two men and to follow them should they leave. They have a brief description of them, so if this information is leaked there are only a few officers who could be responsible. I think I can be confident in my people.'

Denison replied, 'Yes, sir. I understand, but I cannot help hoping it is not one of my team either.'

'Quite understandable, Denison. "We shall see what we shall see," as I'm sure someone once said.' Pallister smiled to himself.

Denison raised an eyebrow but just said, 'Yes, we certainly shall, sir. Thank you, Chief Superintendent. I'll get our plan in motion straight away.'

Chapter Ten

After some hours, two suspects were reported to have left the Eccles address in a hurry. They had piled into the dark red car, with "new" registration plates, and drove off. The constable in plain clothes watching them phoned the waiting unmarked police vehicle, a white van, which duly followed the pair. The officer then phoned the Chief Superintendent.

'Chief Pallister speaking.'

'Sir, Constable Aamir here. The two guys you fingered have just quit the premises, in a hurry.'

'Ah, excellent. Are they being followed, Constable Aamir?' asked Chief Superintendent Pallister.

'Yes, sir. Our van is following. The traffic is heavy so they cannot move very quickly. Is there anything else you wish me to do?'

'No, no, just return to your normal duties. Thank you,' said Pallister.

'Very well, sir.' Aamir rang off. 'A feather in my cap, I hope,' he smiled to himself.

Pallister phoned Denison with an update.

'Hello, Denison speaking.'

'Pallister here. The two are on the move. Obviously, someone has alerted them. Better set your plan in motion.'

'Yes, sir, I certainly will. I'll let you know the result.' Denison rang off and spoke to D.S. Loan. 'Mary, the informer has swallowed the bait. The two killers, Malone and Harvey, are on the move. Let's hope the tail doesn't lose them. Call our four D.Cs. in.'

***

Sid Malone commented as he was driving, 'That was a close one, Jakey boy. That warning came just in time, mate.'

'Yes, it did, and I don't want to worry you, Sid, but there appears to be a van tailing us,' Harvey said as he glanced in the door mirror.

'What? Are you sure?' exclaimed Malone, glancing in the rear-view mirror.

'Yep. It has turned behind us at the last three corners, so I'm pretty certain,' said Harvey. 'There are two blokes in it.'

'Hmm, I will have to shake them off then. Hold onto your hat,' Malone said. He speeded up, and when there was a block in the traffic between them and the following van, he did several quick direction changes.

***

D.Cs. Young, Potter, Kelly and Johnston crowded into Denison's office. They were hoping for good news. The officers in the main office looked on as it was obvious something important was happening.

'Right, take a seat. There has been a development in the Malone/Harvey case,' Denison said as he closed the door. The four looked keen.

'However, that is the good news. The bad news is they were tipped off by an accomplice in our midst.' Four faces fell. They looked at each other mystified.

'You mean a cop tipped them off, sir?' asked Sandra Johnston.

'You think it was one of us!' exclaimed Potter.

'I'm afraid so,' Denison said. 'I want your mobile phones on my desk, now.'

'Our phones? Surely, you cannot...' Sam Potter gasped. The other three looked equally perplexed.

'Phones, here, now,' said Denison tapping his desk.

The four mobile phones were placed on the desk by the detectives.

'What 'bout D.S. Loan's, sorr?' Kelly looked askance at Loan. His accent was more pronounced than usual.

'She has already given me hers,' said Denison, and he placed the fifth phone on the desk. 'Mary, will you call young Wartonberry from the technical department, please?'

Ten minutes later, Stephen Wartonberry entered the office. 'You wanted me, sir?' he said. He was nicknamed "the boffin" as he was a real whizz-kid with anything electronic. He had been since he was six and dismantled and rebuilt his grandmother's old 1950s' wireless set.

'Yes, Stephen, will you examine these five phones and see if any has been used to phone the Manchester area in the past few hours or so? Use that knowhow of yours to see if a call or text has been deleted.'

'Yes, sir, no problem.' Wartonberry sat down at a table, pushed his glasses up with an index finger, picked up the first phone, asked for the password and proceeded to check the phone carefully. He used a computer program to check if any calls or texts had been deleted.

'This is diabolical, sir,' protested Potter.

'I agree with Sam,' said D.C. Emily Young. 'This is totally out of order.'

"Out of order", sir,' snapped Denison looking stern. He was in no mood for insubordination.

D.C. Young repeated, 'This is totally out of order, **sir**.'

After about fifteen or twenty minutes, during which everyone sat or stood looking angry and uncomfortable, Wartonberry placed the last phone back on the desk.

'Well, did you find anything?' asked Denison.

'Nothing, except for a text sent on this one,' he picked up a Motorola phone, 'to a number, to a person called Foxy. There is a strange message: could be a code, sir,' said Wartonberry.

'What does it say?' demanded Denison, as he leaned forward.

'It says: "Foxy, u can xpect visitors v soon. U need to get moving,"' Wartonberry replied.

'Whose phone is this?' Denison almost shouted as he took if from Wartonberry and held it up.

'Erm, that's mine actually, sir' said D.C. Potter, looking faintly amused.

'This is not funny, Potter,' said Denison. 'What does this text mean? Who is this Foxy? Is it code for Malone?'

Potter cleared his throat, paused for effect, and said, 'She is my wife, sir, a nickname as in "Foxy Lady", the song. I was telling her that my parents are arriving for tea as arranged, and to get everything spick and span. My parents tend to be critical if all is not "shipshape and Bristol fashion", sir. My dad was

Royal Navy, and our house, with three kids rampaging, is usually chaotic.' The other D.Cs. smirked. 'I usually text for quickness as my missus does a lot of gardening.'

'You mean…that is all? This has all been a complete waste of time?' D.I. Denison spluttered. D.S. Loan looked disappointed, too.

'Someone could have used a landline, sir,' Wartonberry offered.

'That has already been checked. No calls were made to the Manchester area at that time. Okay, Wartonberry, you may go. Not a word of this to anyone, understand?' Denison's face was almost crimson with embarrassment. 'That goes for you lot too!'

'No, of course not, sir,' Wartonberry said, stifling a grin as he packed up his equipment. *This will be a good laugh at tea break,* he was thinking. He hurried out before he burst out laughing.

Denison knew that the news of his "plan" would spread quicker than melted butter.

'So, we, your team, sorr, have been suspected of being informers for da murderers of our colleagues, sorr,' D.C. Kelly said angrily. 'Dis is a Union matter.' The others murmured agreement.

'Yes, and I apologise profusely. I had to try to find the leak,' said Denison. 'The two criminals have been tipped off twice now, by someone, somewhere. I'm extremely pleased and relieved it is not one of you. Manchester Met. restricted the number of officers involved, so we are no further on.'

'Well, I suppose, sir,' said D.C. Sam Potter with a mischievous smile, 'if you were to stand a round, or even two, of double brandies or large single malt whiskies in the Foxy, erm, Fox and Hounds this evening, sir, we might just overlook it?' He loved the joke, but he kept a straight face. 'My parents will be leaving about seven, so let's say seven thirty at the pub. I'll get a babysitter and bring my missus.'

'Me too,' said D.C. Kelly. 'My missus, dat is, not yours,' he laughed.

'Okay, the drinks are on me. See you at seven thirty,' said Denison, and they all laughed and left. *Maybe I should have specified spouses only or they could bring hundreds,* Denison thought.

Chapter Eleven

Monday, January 23rd

'Well, I hope you have all recovered from Saturday night's boozing session?' Nods and smiles from the squad gathered in Denison's office implied yes. 'Make the most of it as it is unlikely to happen again…ever,' Denison said with a grin. His newly trimmed moustache moved winsomely.

'Aw, sir,' the team chorused and laughed.

'Not a bad old stick,' D.C. Potter murmured.

'Again, I must apologise for putting you through that phone business. It was, unfortunately, necessary. We must plug the leak. Someone is keeping Malone and Harvey informed of every move we make. First, the fake curate is texted, and now they were warned that we knew their whereabouts in Eccles. This was a trap set by the Chief Superintendent in Manchester and has excluded the Manchester cops from any suspicion. Any ideas would be welcome.' Denison looked around the team, Some were sitting, some standing.

'The leak must be in Manchester, sir. There are a lot more officers so easier to escape detection,' D.S. Loan insisted.

'Yes, Mary,' said Denison, 'but the Chief Super. there made sure he let only necessary trusted people know the plan.

The constable watching the hideout did not know their names. Just to look for two men leaving.'

D.C. Kelly said, 'He or she, da informer, could not have known da hideout was being watched, sorr, so dey were not in da Chief's inner circle, so to speak.'

'Which begs the question: how did they get the info?' said Denison. 'Only Mary and I knew of the plan at this end.'

The others looked in Mary Loan's direction. 'Don't look at me!' she cried, holding up her hands. 'I never called them.'

'Someone on the switchboard listening in, sir?' suggested D.C. Potter.

'Nah, too hit and miss. Bound to be dozens of operators so the chances of a mole picking up anything is negligible,' said Denison. He sighed and studied the incident board for inspiration. *There is a leak somewhere, but where is it?* he wondered. 'The answer is there somewhere.' He led them to the incident board. Blank faces stared at it.

***

'Another fine mess you've got me into, Jakey,' Sid Malone did a passable imitation of Oliver Hardy.

'I got you into! Me?! Who was it that said: "That woman cop has clocked your mug. We'll have to get rid of them"? That was you, Sidney Malone! It was your idea.' Jacob Harvey responded angrily. 'The police will never rest from investigating the deaths of two of their own.'

'Okay, okay, but I'm sure they were about to report seeing you that night in your digs in Edward Street. We had no choice. None,' Malone responded. 'The bloke was on the phone.'

'Lucky that old boat had passed by and attracted their attention, or they would have been more alert,' said Harvey. 'That train crossing the bridge helped cover any noise. Couldn't have timed it better. We were able to get right up to them without being spotted.'

'Yeah, always liked trains and them canal boats. I like them even more now,' Malone laughed.

'What did you do with the old golf clubs?' Harvey asked.

'Chucked them in the river while you fetched the car, didn't I?' said Malone.

'What if they search the river and find them, eh?' Harvey looked worried.

'So, what if they do? No prints or nothing. Just two old clubs as was lying about under the stairs in the house. Hadn't been used in years by the looks of them, and I'm sure they won't be missed,' Malone replied.

'Yes, but they were under the stairs where I lived! So, now we are stuck in Castlewood, back where we started. We pulled that post office job in Manchester and were just going to lie low for a few months, so I got that curate's job as a cover. "We'll soon be sunning ourselves in Spain," you said,' said Harvey. 'So, where are we now? Doesn't look much like Spain from where I'm sitting! Doesn't smell like Spain neither!' He sniffed the air.

'In my friend's garage for the time being. Pongs a bit, I agree, and it's none too comfortable,' replied Malone, groaning as he shifted some old car parts from where he was sitting.

The garage was situated at the back of the house, halfway down the garden. It had not been used for years, as the car the householder, McClean, owned was extra-large to accommodate his bulk.

'I meant, what do we do now with every cop in the country looking for us? If it hadn't been for that what's-the-name you know, we would have been nabbed ages ago. I just managed to get away in the nick of time from the cathedral office when they texted,' Harvey added.

'Yeah, S…oops, I'll not say the word.' Malone put a hand over his mouth.

'Their name starts with an *S*?' asked Harvey.

Malone shrugged, 'Might be a name, might be a nickname. It doesn't matter. My informant has come in handy. Best you don't know who they are so you cannot be forced to blab, Jakey,' said Malone.

'I won't ever grass to the "Old Bill". You know me better than that,' Harvey replied, feeling peeved.

'Still, it's best you don't know…

'You were pretty useless as a curate anyway. I thought you said you knew a bit o' the Bible,' Malone jibed.

'Well, I thought I did. Went to Sunday school when I was a nipper, didn't I, but I have forgotten most of it.' Harvey chuckled as he recalled, 'I was telling the kids about Bethlehem and that, on Christmas Eve, and what did I do? I said Jesus's mum was called Marge. I mixed her up with *The Simpsons* for some reason. They all burst out laughing, then the whole congregation burst out laughing. I felt a right twit. Fortunately, the bishop and dean thought I had done it deliberately for a joke to amuse the children, and I got away with it.'

'You certainly would not have lasted much longer there, that's for sure. And why did you hide that student's body in a freezer? Why did you not bury it somewhere, where it would never be found?' Malone asked.

'Didn't have a spade, did I? Anyway, there were students all over the place. There was no way I could sneak a dead body out unseen.' Harvey asserted. He mimicked a posh voice, '"I say, what's that you're carrying, old chap? Looks like a dead body!" "Oh, this? It's only my washing I'm taking to the laundrette!"' They both laughed.

Harvey continued, 'What we need are two passports and a wad of cash to get us out of the country. South of Spain or West Indies would be nice. Plenty of sunshine. Hawaii even.'

Malone grunted. 'First, we have only about five hundred and fifty quid between us. That post office job was a disaster, especially after you dropped a sack of cash while we were making a getaway and the wind blew it all over the street. And second, the cops will be watching every port and airport like hawks. We killed two coppers, remember? Not to mention that creep Billy and the student. No way will they give up. There is no way we could get away even with fake passports. We will just have to lie low for a few months. Besides, it would take a small fortune to pay Freddy the Forger to supply them. He won't come cheap.'

'Well, if we just have to squat here for a while longer ask your mate for a heater at least. I'm perished. My toes are numb,' Harvey moaned. He stood up and flapped his arms around his body and stamped his feet to try to warm up.

'Okay, but I don't want to push him too much or he might just tell us to clear off,' Malone replied, and he went to the rear door of the house to have a word with the owner, one Alex "Grizzly Bear" McClean, a great hairy hulk of a man, a professional wrestler. Arms and legs like tree trunks, and a body that required clothes specifically tailored. He had a full black beard and long hair in a ponytail. He made the legendary "Giant Haystacks" and "Big Daddy" look tiny.

'Sorry to disturb you again, Grizzly, but we are freezing out in the garage. Do you have a heater we could use?' Malone smiled his friendliest smile and flapped his arms around him to emphasise the need to keep warm.

'Hmm, suppose I could,' McClean grumbled. 'I'd let you stay in the house only the missus won't hear of it. "If they get caught in the garage, we can deny all knowledge," she said, so you will have to stay there. How long for, by the way? If it's a long time you'll have to cough up a few quid for the 'lectricity. It doesn't come cheap these days. I don't earn a lot with me wrestling bouts.'

'It won't be for long, mate. We are hoping to skip off to Spain or someplace, soon as,' said Malone. 'We just need some readies, cash like.'

'Hmm. Okay then. You can borrow that little 'lectric fire there.' He pointed to a small two-bar fire in a corner. 'Don't be burning it all day and night though,' McClean warned. 'The missus will go crazy if she finds out. Me life won't be worth living. I'll sneak a couple more blankets out to you when she goes shopping. She's still snoring, at the moment.' Regular noises could be heard from upstairs to confirm this. 'And there are a couple of old sleeping bags somewhere if the missus hasn't chucked them out. Forever clearing stuff out, she is. Threw out my favourite trainers, she did, just because there was a hole in the sole of one. Ponged a bit too, I must admit.' McClean laughed.

'Big lad like you should be able to stand up to your missus,' Malone replied, laughing.

'You've met her! Could you stand up to her in one of her moods?' McClean winced. 'I'd rather fight ten blokes at the same time in the ring than argue with my missus.' He shuddered.

'Erm, maybe not. I'll keep out of her way, to be on the safe side,' said Malone. 'We'll be very economical, we will. And blankets and sleeping bags will be very welcome. Thanks, Grizzly.' And he returned to the garage.

'Is that wee heater all you could get? It's minute. No way that will heat this whole garage,' Harvey complained.

'Quit your moaning. Moan, moan, moan is all you ever do. Worse than my ex-wife. And we cannot burn it 24/7 either. Grizzly will want payment otherwise, and he will get us some blankets and possibly sleeping bags,' Malone replied. 'And I remind you, we are nearly skint. Beggars can't be choosers. We could put a blanket up across part of the garage to make a smaller space to heat.'

'Better than nothing, I suppose,' said Harvey, and he wrapped another coat around his shoulders.

Chapter Twelve

'Right, troops,' said Denison, 'the two blokes we are looking for have gone to ground somewhere. They have not escaped out of the country, I'm certain of that. The Home Secretary has ordered extra staff to be at airports and seaports around the clock. A dormouse couldn't slip through.'

'Nor a couple of snakes,' Emily Young added. They all smiled.

'So, can we assume they may still be either in Manchester or Castlewood, sir?' asked D.C. Johnston.

'Yes, but where? That's the problem. Manchester is too hot for them, as they will know they were informed on by some rival gang, so it is quite possible they are here in Castlewood. I want every available copper, community support officers, and volunteers searching every house and shed in the city, which is comparatively small, thankfully. Take staff off office duties if necessary. In fact, I insist on it. The Chief Constable has authorised it. If they are here, we will find them; we must find them before they murder anyone else,' Denison vowed. 'I'll see if I can get some army help too. Mary, get the local barracks on the phone, please. Colonel Brookfield is the C.O.'

'Okay, sir, I'll get that all organised straight away. I think Manchester, as you said, would be too hot for them, so assuming they have not gone further afield, they must be here somewhere,' D.S. Loan replied.

'Right, let's get a map and divide the city into sectors. It's hard to say if they will be in the centre or the suburbs, so we'll start in the city centre and work outwards,' Denison decided.

And so, later that day, blocks of the city were cordoned off by the police and the search began. Many citizens were annoyed at the disruption but had to suffer the inconvenience. Roadblocks to prevent the two from escaping were set up and every vehicle was searched by police officers and volunteers. A helicopter circled over the fields in the area.

***

'Oi, you two loafers, you had better be on your toes out of here,' growled Grizzly McClean that afternoon, 'the peelers are searching every house, so they will be doing this place in a matter of hours. Cops and soldiers everywhere. You can't move in town for coppers.'

His wife was standing behind him, hair in curlers, arms akimbo, and scowling. 'And they are searching all vehicles leaving the city, so hop it,' she growled. She looked more frightening than Grizzly.

'Searching? That's all we need,' said Malone. 'Okay, give us a minute to get our kit together and we'll scarper.' The two threw their few belongings into a couple of bags and legged it. The car, deemed a liability, had been abandoned earlier in an alley a mile away.

'How are we going to get out of town, Sid?' Jake Harvey asked.

'How should I know? We will try to get into an area they have already searched and lie low again, until opportunity knocks, Jakey,' said Malone. 'Don't worry, I know this city like the back of my hand.'

'I certainly hope so,' Harvey muttered, looking at Malone's veiny hand. He was extremely worried.

And so, using his knowledge of every alley and sewer, Malone managed to find another hideout with an old pal in the city centre.

'Cor! You two don't half pong,' their new host commented, holding his nose.

'Had to come through a few sewers, didn't we?' said Malone with a grin.

The host replied, 'Okay, help yourselves to the shower and bung your togs in the washing machine. I'll lend you some of mine. They should fit okay.

'The cops have been through this street with a magnifying glass, guys, so it's unlikely they will return. Give me a few quid and I'll fetch food. Our cupboards are nearly empty because the wife hasn't gone shopping yet.

'You can use the old granny-flat at the back. Keep the blinds closed. No lights at night or nosey neighbours might see. Some of them would tattle to the cops, no bother,' said their host Joe Walsh nicknamed "the Chief" as he was once a gang leader. He preferred the quiet life now, almost being legal. He kept his hand in with an occasional fell-off-the-back-of-a-lorry item of value.

'I hope your missus doesn't mind,' said Malone.

'Nah, she won't care. Just don't spill anything on the new carpet.' He made a gesture of a knife across his throat and laughed.

***

'Looks like the pair have given us the slip, again,' Denison declared. He slumped back in his chair.

'Should we start the search over again, sir?' asked D.S. Loan.

'No, no, the public won't stand for it. Social media is already full of stuff about how we are "blighting their lives" and such,' Denison replied, miming quotation marks with his fingers. 'Besides, Harris, the Chief Superintendent, has ruled out another search on financial grounds. In other words, the budget is blown.'

As if by good timing John Harris, the big cheese of Castlewood, stuck his head around the door. 'Any success with the search?'

'No, sir, a complete waste of time, almost. We did find the hoards of stolen property of at least three thieves. Gold watches, war medals, silver photo frames. You name it, they have it. Right lot of little Fagins they are,' said Denison. 'There were even half a dozen Rolls Royce car emblems…that woman with the wings, or whatever it is supposed to be.'

'Hmm, that's something anyway, I suppose,' Harris replied.

'Lost Property are going to be busy for a while,' D.S. Loan commented.

'Yes, they will. So, what's next, Denison?' Harris asked.

'It is possible, of course, that they are long gone from here, sir, But I have a gut feeling they are still in hiding, with some crony of Malone's. He is bound to have cronies. And my gut is rarely wrong,' he laughed, patting his belly. The detectives smiled but said nothing.

'Right, I'll be off. Round of golf with the Lord Mayor,' Harris said and smiled.

'Well for some,' D.C. Potter muttered as Harris disappeared down the corridor.

'Exactly. Chiefs play golf while we slog our guts out,' said Denison. 'I hope I get a promotion soon,' he laughed.

Chapter Thirteen

Sunday, January 29th

'I've been for a drive around, and the cops are only stopping the occasional vehicle now, as the locals are complaining about the restrictions,' said Joe Walsh. 'They must be thinking you two have left town already. So, this is what I suggest: you two dress up as two old ladies in black, mourning like, and if we are stopped, I'll say we are going to a funeral. Easy peasy.'

'What if they ask questions?' Harvey asked looking dubious.

'You do a lot of crying and wailing and such. And be sure to shave! You look like a couple of pirates,' replied Walsh. The two fugitives had not shaved for days.

That afternoon a car with a driver and three passengers drove out of town. Walsh was driving, wearing a black suit and tie; his wife, Elsie, also dressed in black, sat in the front passenger seat and two distraught "ladies" were in the back. The two fugitives were wearing wigs and black ladies' coats and hats borrowed for the occasion. Lots of makeup and handkerchiefs dabbing eyes hid traces of facial hair.

At the city boundary on the Burton road, a police officer stepped into the road and raised his hand. Walsh slowed down and stopped.

'What can I do for you, Constable?' asked Walsh.

The police officer glanced in at the passengers. Harvey let out a convincing high-pitched wail and buried his face in a handkerchief. 'May I ask your name, address, and where you are going, sir?'

'Joe Walsh of 16, South Street. Just off to a funeral in Burton-upon-Trent, Officer. These dear ladies' brother has snuffed it, erm, "shuffled off this mortal toil, erm, coil", I mean,' Walsh replied. Malone wailed loudly. *Don't overdo it, Sid,* Walsh thought. 'There, there, Daisy, don't be upset,' he said over his shoulder.

'Hmm,' the constable looked in again. 'Okay, proceed. Sorry for your loss, ladies.' The two in the back seat nodded their thanks. The car drove on. The occupants breathed a sigh of relief.

The officer scratched his head. 'I could swear I smelt men's aftershave on those ladies.'

'Never use it myself, so I wouldn't know,' said another.

'Perhaps it was the driver's,' said the first officer.

Further down the road, the two fugitives relaxed again and let out whoops of joy. 'You played a blinder, Joe,' said Malone.

Joe replied, 'I thought you were auditioning for an Oscar, man.'

***

'Looks like the two killers have definitely given us the slip,' Denison said. 'There has been no sign of them for days now.'

'They must have got out of the city somehow, sir,' said D.S. Loan.

'I want you to contact all your informers, and double, no treble, the reward for information leading to an arrest,' Denison said, looking grim.

'I hope it brings some results, sorr,' said D.C. Kelly.

'The longer the trail is cold, the more difficult it will be to trace them,' said D.C. Young.

'Right, off you go and get your "snitches" sniffing around,' Denison urged.

The detectives headed off into the haunts of the local underworld. Bars, snooker halls and various dives were visited in turn. There was still a wariness of speaking to the police because of what happened to Billy Bowler.

'More than my life's worth to tell you anything,' was a common response.

Chapter Fourteen

Friday, February 3rd

'Sir, one of my snitches, Wally Mulgrew, a usually dependable chap, has told me that Malone and Harvey have moved to Burton-upon-Trent,' D.C. Sandra Johnston said, almost unable to contain her excitement. 'They apparently escaped in a car pretending to be old women going to a funeral. At least that is what Mulgrew claims. How he found that out is anybody's guess.'

'Hmm, great news. Tongues wag even in the criminal circles. We can assume that they are no longer dressed as old women,' Denison chuckled. The detectives laughed too. 'I'll get on the blower to Burton's Chief Superintendent straight away. Good work, Sandra,' said Denison, and he lifted a telephone.

'Sir, D.I. Walter Denison here from Castlewood C.I.D.'

'Ah, Denison, not heard from you in ages. How's your wife? Last I heard she was in hospital, old chap,' the Chief Superintendent, Claude Simpson, said.

'Oh, she's fine now, sir, thanks. Still bossing me around,' Denison chuckled.

'Good, good. You found those two killers yet, Denison?'

'That's why I called you, sir. Word on the street is they are holed up over there in Burton somewhere,' Denison replied.

'Hmm, are they indeed? I haven't heard anything this end. Well, any help you need just ask,' Simpson said.

'If I may, sir, I would like to bring my team over there and operate from your station. It would be much handier. Better to be on the spot if anything turns up.'

'Yes, yes, it is unusual but no problem. My folk are busy chasing a suspected terrorist gang, so I'll have some office space cleared for you. If I am able to, I'll also round up a couple of detectives to assist you. How does that sound?'

'Sounds great, sir. We will be there this afternoon if that is suitable,' said Denison.

'Excellent, old chap. See you all later. Give my best wishes to your wife. Bye,' the Chief said.

'I will indeed, sir. Bye, for now.' Denison hung up. He turned to his squad as Samantha Nixon from pathology, appeared at the office door.

'Excuse me, sir, just to let you know, the bodies of your colleagues are released for burial. Shall I contact the next of kin?'

'No, I'll do that myself. It's my responsibility. Thanks, Samantha,' Denison said, looking sad. He continued, 'Right, pack a toothbrush, troops. We are off to Burton. I'll just have a word with our boss about arranging the funerals and about going to Burton, visit the two families, which fortunately are local, and then we shall depart for pastures new.

'Oh and get your uniforms out of the wardrobe ready for the funerals.'

***

'Just got word from my contact that the Castlewood cops are coming here to town,' Malone said to their current host, Charlie "the Ferret" Jones. Not because he resembled a ferret but because he was always "ferreting" around for ill-gotten gains. Anything illegal that would show a profit. He was a local lowlife in Burton -upon -Trent.

'How did they trace us?' asked Jake Harvey in despair.

'Some rat has probably grassed on us,' Sid Malone declared. 'My contact didn't know.'

'Yeah, most likely,' said Jones. 'Not to worry, lads, you are safe here. At least for a while. Nobody but me and the wife knows where you are, and woe betide anyone here who dares go to the police.'

'That's some comfort anyway, Jonesy,' said Malone. 'We are a bit low on readies at present, but we will repay you soon as, mate.'

'Don't you worry about that. We go back a long way, we do. The Young Offenders' Centre in Lichfield, wasn't it?'

'It sure was, Jonesy. The "House of Correction" they called it. It was like something out of Oliver Twist. I was a bad lad back then, still am I suppose,' Malone laughed.

'You got that right. Didn't correct either of you,' Harvey laughed. 'We really appreciate what you are doing for us, Jonesy.'

'Think nothing of it. You are quite safe in this here cellar. No one around here knows it exists. It must have been blocked off decades ago by a previous owner for some reason. Perhaps there is a ghost haunting it.'

'A what?!' Harvey exclaimed. 'I'm not staying…'

Malone laughed, 'He is only pulling your leg, you idiot.'

'Well, okay,' Harvey nodded. He was of a nervous disposition. He hated scary films.

Jones resumed, 'I only uncovered the entrance by chance when I was renovating. A bit of carpet and a few boxes over it and you wouldn't know it was there. Perfect!'

Jones' large townhouse was in its own grounds overlooking the river. It dated from the eighteenth century. Extensive gardens and shrubbery ensured a deal of privacy from prying eyes.

Chapter Fifteen

Tuesday, February 7th

During the day, Malone and Harvey were able to walk and exercise in the enclosed garden at the back of the house. The weather was cold but dry. Then they retired to the cellar at night. Jones piled boxes over the entrance to the hideout just in case of unwelcome visitors. There were no windows to show a light outside, so they avoided being totally in the dark. Fresh air came through a ventilation brick and a duct from the hallway above them.

Malone said, 'Those Castlewood detectives working from Burton police headquarters are going to cause us problems, Jake.'

'Yeah, that Inspector Denison is no fool. Might be Walter but he is no wally. But there is no way he can find us here, I hope,' Harvey replied.

'True, but I don't want to spend the rest of my days in this cellar. Jonesy is a good mate but, sooner or later, he is going to want his house back. And we are still short of money.'

'What are you thinking, Sid?' Harvey wondered.

'We need money, lots of lovely money…in untraceable notes.'

'Hmm, true enough. Cannot deny that.'

'And where do you find lots of money?' asked Malone.

'Erm, a gold mine?' Harvey replied.

'Bit short of gold mines around Staffordshire, my friend.' Malone replied. 'But there is a nice juicy bank ripe for plucking on the main street: "The Burton Savings and Investment Bank Ltd". They are loaded, I'm sure. Enough to serve our needs anyway.

'I recall scouting it out a half dozen years ago with a view to robbing it. I was with Willie Metcalf and Johnny Rogers back then, but the two of them were lifted for another job and got fifteen years. You are too young to have known them.'

'Hmm. Bad luck that,' commented Harvey, smiling.

'Well, all is not lost. I can remember the inside security cameras and stuff. Assuming they have not been changed, I think we might just pick up where we left off, Jake, old chum.'

'Oh, right. I have only done a bank job once before. Could be tricky enough,' Harvey said.

'It will take a lot of careful planning for sure. I'll get some paper and pens from Charlie and sketch what I can remember,' said Malone. 'It's an old bank so, hopefully, the safe is antique and easily opened.'

For an hour, Malone worked at his drawing, tongue out of one side of his mouth as he concentrated. He sat back to admire his work and nodded. 'A work of art, that,' he murmured. He had drawn out a detailed plan of the bank, as it was when he was last in it. CCTV cameras, doorways and windows, where the safe was, as far as he could guess, remembering the manager coming and going, were all marked.

'Good work, there, Sid,' said Jones, 'and I shall pay it a visit tomorrow to lodge some cash and see if there have been any major changes.' Jones studied every detail of the drawing.

'Good idea, Jonesy,' said Harvey. 'Then all we have to do is come up with a plan.'

'It will take a lot of planning. I may be a bit rusty at the safe-cracking now, but I am sure the safe will be a piece of cake,' Jones said. Malone grinned.

***

Wednesday, February 8th

The bank was prominent in the main street: a large, imposing edifice approached by a flight of steps to a portico with four sturdy pillars with Doric capitals, and a pediment decorated with allegorical figures of Thrift, Industry, Wealth, Plenty and Progress.

Charlie Jones, smartly dressed, paid a visit to the said bank, pretending to open an account to deposit a small sum. He spent some minutes carefully and slowly filling out a lodgement slip for a new account. No relevant detail of the bank's interior escaped his notice. He was wearing tinted spectacles so he could look around without arousing suspicion.

While the bank clerk, Miss Belling, was filling in forms to open an account, Jones glanced around the room mentally noting details of the security. He noticed a steel shutter had been installed over the tellers' counters. In an emergency, this would drop down sealing the staff off from a robbery. He guessed the front door would be locked at the same time.

'Well, Mr Smith, that is all the paperwork completed. Have you any identification, sir? Just a formality; a driving licence, for example,' Miss Belling said, smiling sweetly.

Charlie Jones, wearing a grey wig and false grey beard, using a walking stick, looked surprised. 'Oh, identification? Oh, goodness, I never thought that would be needed. Let me see,' he searched his pockets. 'No, sorry. I have nothing with me, Miss. What a to-do. I am a silly billy.'

'I'm afraid regulations require something to verify your identity, Mr Smith,' the clerk replied. 'A gas bill, or electricity bill?'

'Hmm, hold on to these papers and I'll nip home, get something and come straight back. It's not far,' Jones said, and he left. He, of course, had no intention of returning. A hundred metres down the street, he dumped the stick and wig in a waste bin when nobody was looking.

'Well, lads, it is pretty much as Sid remembers it, except for a steel security shutter. But as we shall probably make our withdrawal after closing time it will hardly signify.' Jones grinned as he reported back to the others.

'"We"? "Our"?' said Malone. 'Are you joining us, Jonesy?'

'I certainly am, Sid, if you'll have me. It's a long time since I did a bit of safecracking. I miss the adrenalin rush. So, let's get the ball rolling,' Jones rubbed his hands together. 'Should be a piece of cake. Like taking candy from a baby.'

'Yep, this is going to be some caper,' said Harvey.

Malone grinned from ear to ear. Or what was left of his right ear as a piece had been bitten off in a fight when he was a teen.

Chapter Sixteen

Friday, February 10th

'Good morning, Mrs Carling, might I have a word, please?' said Miss Belling the teller in the bank.

'Yes, certainly, Carol. Good morning,' the supervisor replied. She was an excellent boss but insisted on the full expression: no "Morning" for her. She detested shortened words like phone, TV or bike. She always used a cup and saucer for her tea; never a mug and her only concession to convenience was using teabags. And definitely no sugar. But her staff adored her.

'It's just that an elderly man was in on Wednesday and wanted to open an account. He had no identification and said he was going home to get something. He still has not returned. There is no telephone number listed; I checked the directory, so what should I do with this application?'

Mrs Carling looked at the application form. 'Hmm, he lives only a few streets away, so there is no reason why he could not have returned by now. Perhaps he changed his mind or been knocked down by a bus.' Miss Belling would have laughed had her supervisor been the type of person to make a joke. 'If he has not returned by closing time today file it in the waste bin, Carol.' Mrs Carling said with a straight face.

'Yes, I will do that, Mrs Carling. Thank you,' Miss Belling replied, suppressing a chuckle. 'I can always redo it should he return.'

Mrs Carling strode off to make sure everything was prepared for the day's business.

***

The three would-be bank-robbers had spent the time since Wednesday making meticulous plans.

'So, are we all agreed that we knock out the CCTV in the yard behind the bank, get one of us, you Jake being the smallest, in through that small window beside the rear entrance?' said Malone. They had secretly taken some photographs. 'I'm handy with a catapult. I've been practising so the camera should not be a problem.' A quantity of bashed baked bean cans in the garden were proof of that.

'What if the window is alarmed? It's bound to be alarmed or have an iron bar fitted,' said Harvey. He was beginning to have second thoughts about the whole affair.

'We knock out the electricity supply at a suitable point. That will silence any alarm,' Jones replied. 'We shall just have to take the chance that it is not barred. I had a quick look at it a couple of days ago and I could not see any.'

'Right, let's go over it once more,' said Malone. They spread the map on a table.

Jones cleared his throat noisily and started. 'We park the car here,' he pointed to a narrow street on the map, 'behind the National Brewery Centre. Then we take this alley to the back of the bank. There are no dwellings so it should be deserted. I nobble the power line, here. That will put the whole block in darkness. It will take time for it to be repaired, being late at night. Sid will then take out the camera with his catapult,' he chuckled. 'Okay so far?' The others nodded hesitantly. 'Next, we break in through the window beside the back entrance. You are like a beanpole, Jake, so you should be able to squeeze in and open the door for us two.'

'What if they have a backup electricity supply and the cameras come on? We will be recognised easily,' Harvey said.

'We wear these masks, like Zorro.' Jones pulled three black eye-masks from a pocket.

'Wow, you've thought of everything, dude,' Malone said admiringly.

'I certainly hope so or we will be in difficulties,' Jones said. 'I got a glimpse of the safe in a back office when the manager opened the door. It looks old, Dickensian actually, and it should not take me more than a few minutes to crack it.'

'A man of many talents, Charlie,' said Harvey. Jones laughed.

'Right, let's sleep on it and tomorrow night we do a practice run. Okay?' Jones said.

'Sure thing,' said Malone. He yawned.

'Maybe we should wait for the Easter bank holiday when it will be closed for longer?' Harvey asked.

'Nah, too far away. Besides, we will be in and out in a jiffy. It isn't the Hatton Garden job,' Jones laughed.

Chapter Seventeen

Saturday, February 11th. Two a.m. on a wintry night

As soon as the town quietened down after revellers had gone home, and much of the traffic had departed, the three would-be bank robbers drove to the proposed street and parked within a few metres of the National Brewery Centre, a museum of old brewing equipment and techniques. It was beside an existing brewery. A few snowflakes fluttered down. All was quiet.

Jones said, 'Right, we shall walk at a leisurely pace to the back of the bank. Jake, make a note of the time it takes. If there are any people about just keep walking and we will try another night.'

'Yeah, no problem,' Harvey replied. They set off.

Arriving at the back of the bank, a security gate of iron bars was secured with a padlock and topped by razor wire.

'You never mentioned razor wire,' said Malone.

'It's not a problem. I can open that lock in about ten seconds,' Jones replied. 'Are you sure you can hit the CCTV camera, Sid?'

Malone peered through the bars. 'Easy as falling off a log, mate.'

'Okay,' said Jones. 'I cannot see that window being a problem. Jakey should get through it easily. We had better not hang about too long tonight. Don't wish to arouse suspicions.' The three retraced their steps to the car. They all climbed in and sat for a while chatting.

'When is the next moonless night, or as nearly moonless as possible?' Malone asked.

Jones replied, 'Next Wednesday, the fifteenth, looks a likely night. I looked it up on the internet. Besides, there is a big match at the football ground, Burton Albion F.C. versus West Bromwich Albion in the Cup. Burton plays Brighton and Hove Albion in the next round if they win.'

'That's a lot of "Albions",' Harvey joked.

'Lots of cops will be required there, especially as I have arranged for a mini riot to occur!' Jones grinned.

'Oh, nice,' commented Malone, grinning. 'Love a good riot, me!'

Jones continued, 'I have let it be known, anonymously of course, that trouble is expected, so the police force will be out in force. Excuse the pun.'

'Well, okay, Wednesday evening it is, barring anything unexpected,' said Malone.

'Can't wait,' said Harvey, rubbing his hands.

***

Wednesday, February 15ᵗʰ

The match kicked off at 7:30 p.m. and the "riot" was set to start at eight. The three robbers left Jones' house timed to arrive near the museum some minutes before eight, then parked the car and walked casually to the alley behind the bank. All was quiet, as expected.

They were soon at the back gate of the bank. Jones went to an electricity junction box and twenty seconds later, the district was in darkness. It took some seconds for their eyes to adjust to the darkness. Malone fired his catapult and on the second attempt, smashed the camera in case it had an independent electricity supply. Jones then picked the lock on the gate, and they crept in, closing the gate behind them. Then they proceeded to the little window. Jones jemmied it open and stuck his head and shoulders inside.

'Brilliant, the "on" lights on the cameras are all out, so in you go, Jakey. Put the masks on, guys, just in case. And don't forget your gloves.' They all put on rubber gloves purloined from the local hospital. Jones did not believe in buying things, which could be obtained for free.

Harvey wriggled through the window then opened the rear door for the other two. The three were soon all inside and headed for the office with the safe.

'Jakey, look out of that window at the front street to see if all is quiet, please,' said Jones.

'It's as quiet as a quiet thing,' Harvey joked.

Jones took a deep breath then proceeded to get a stethoscope he had also nicked from the hospital and settled down at the safe. 'Keep a good lookout. Not a sound, lads.' He worked for several minutes turning the combination until he said, 'That's it. We're in. Can't believe they still have this old safe,' and he turned the handle. The other two breathed easily again. He hauled out several bundles of banknotes, mostly twenties and tens, and put them in a bag.

'Must be thousands here, Charlie,' said Malone, flicking a bundle of notes. 'And all untraceable.'

'There certainly is. Enough to get fake passports and you two out of the country, and a cut for me, too,' said Jones. 'By the way, I had to bung a few hundred quid to the rioters.'

'Not a problem. Just add it to your cut. We had better scarper sharpish though before they get the electricity on again,' Malone said. The three checked that they had left nothing behind and exited by the rear door. Jones closed the gate and relocked it. 'That will baffle PC Plod for a while,' he laughed, and they moved quickly back to their vehicle.

Back at Jones' house, they divided the takings and were surprised at how much they had got.

'Wow, a good night's work, lads,' Jones said. 'I'll pick up the passports in the morning. You two had better get down in the cellar, just in case. Take this cash with you. I'll trust you.'

Chapter Eighteen

'Sir,' said D.S. Iain Fitzroy of the Burton Constabulary, inside the bank six hours later, 'it's going back a few years, and he might be dead, but this has the hallmarks of the infamous Charles Jones.'

Detective Chief Superintendent Claude Simpson replied, 'You are not wrong, Iain. This has all the trademarks of his *modus operandi* all right. Explains how they got in at the back gate anyway. He always replaced locks he had picked. Check our records for his last known address.'

Fitzroy typed on a laptop. 'Last address we have is 105, Claremont Heights here in town.'

'Posh area. Who was it said crime doesn't pay?' said the Chief Superintendent sarcastically.

'It says that he has a legit business, an estate agent's, according to this,' Fitzroy added.

'Pigs might fly. Right, two of you constables with me. We shall pay a call on Mr Jones. Any of you guys from Castlewood want to tag along?'

'Yeah sure, why not? Beats twiddling our thumbs here, which we have been doing since we got here,' D.I. Denison said. 'Mary and Sam, you can come too.'

So, D.C.S. Simpson, D.S. Iain Fitzroy, two uniformed constables with D.I. Denison, D.S. Mary Loan and D.C. Sam Potter piled into two cars and headed for Jones' address.

'Some house!' Potter exclaimed as they drove up the paved driveway. 'It must have cost a fortune.' It was indeed huge and secluded. The gate had been opened remotely from the house to allow them in.

They all approached the front door, except for Potter and the constables who went around the back.

Fitzroy rang the bell. Inside, Jones had hurriedly covered the cellar entrance and then opened the door. 'What can I do for you gents, and lady?' he asked slightly out of breath. 'Been doing my exercise routine. Doctor's orders,' he lied.

Simpson introduced himself and the others. 'Jones, have you been up to your old tricks again?' he asked.

'Goodness, whatever do you mean, Officer Simpson?' Jones looked offended. 'What are you now? Carpark attendant?'

Simpson ignored the jibe. 'A bank was done over earlier tonight, and it has your M. O. all over it,' Simpson said.

'*Moi! Mais non, mais non.*' He faked a French accent. 'But I have been a law-abiding citizen for years, ask anybody. They'll vouch for me,' Jones said, looking innocent and shocked. 'I play golf with council bigwigs.'

'Oh, I'm sure there are many who will do that. Where were you at about eight p.m. this evening, Jones?'

'I was here watching TV, wasn't I?'

'Is there anyone to verify that?' asked Simpson.

'I was just about to say, the wife was here. Shall I call her?'

'Yes, please do,' Simpson replied.

'Sarah, can you come here a minute, please? The "Old Bill" wants a word,' Jones shouted and smiled slyly.

Sarah Jones appeared from the kitchen, wiping her hands on a cloth, where she had been preparing a light supper.

'Good evening, Mrs Jones,' said Simpson. 'Can you verify your husband's whereabouts this evening?'

'He has been here all evening, Officer, since he got home from work at six,' she said.

'And he never left the house?' asked the Superintendent.

'No, he did not. Cosy night in. We watched an old film: *The Longest Day* and it is a long film,' Mrs Jones stated. 'He dozed off for a while in the middle of it. Missed the best part.'

'That's true, Officer, I was watching the film with my darling missus.' Jones gazed adoringly at his wife.

'Hmm, do you mind if we take a look around, sir?' said D.S. Fitzroy. 'Just to check nothing is amiss.'

'No, knock yourselves out, even if you have no search warrant. I have nothing to hide,' Jones replied and waved an arm casually towards the living room. He had his fingers crossed in a pocket.

The constables and Potter were called in from the back of the building by Fitzroy, and the police officers spread out and looked around the premises. Fitzroy felt the top of the television set and it was warm.

After about half an hour, they prepared to depart having found nothing. 'Thank you, Mr and Mrs Jones, sorry for disturbing your evening,' said Simpson politely.

D.I. Denison asked suddenly on an impulse, 'Any hidden rooms in the house, by any chance? These old houses often have secret passages and rooms.'

The Joneses glanced at each other but soon recovered their composure. 'Certainly not, Officer,' Jones laughed. 'You're thinking of the seventeenth century. This house is not that old. No secret Cavaliers' hiding places, I'm afraid. Sorry to disappoint,' he grinned.

'Very well, I bid you goodnight,' said Denison and the officers left.

In the car, as they prepared to return to the station, Fitzroy said, 'Did you catch the look that pair gave each other when you mentioned secret hiding places?'

'Yes, there was a frisson of worry there, definitely. We need a search warrant and a return visit as soon as possible,' Denison replied. 'Should have got one before we came here.'

'I'll get one tonight if possible. It might take an hour or two,' D.C.S. Simpson said. 'You two constables can stay on watch here,' he said to the two men.

'Sid and Jake,' Jones called as he removed the boxes from hiding the cellar door. 'You need to scarper quickly because I have the feeling that the cops will be back with a search warrant.'

'I thought they had been satisfied, from what we could hear,' said Malone. The sound travelled down the ventilation shaft from the hallway.

'It's just a gut feeling I have from their reaction. We were taken unawares when he mentioned a secret room. Me and the missus glanced at each other,' Jones replied.

His wife shouted, 'They have left two men at the gate, Charlie! I can see them trying not to be seen.'

'Okay, we are out of here, mate. Jake, grab our gear,' said Malone. Five minutes later, the two exited by a small gate used by the gardener at the bottom of the extensive garden.

The Joneses tidied up the cellar to hide traces of recent use, and then went to bed. The two robbers headed into the night.

'Homeless again,' Jake Harvey moaned.

'Do you know who that copper was, Jake?' Malone asked as they ran.

'Nah, who was it?'

'Only D.I. Denison, that's who. I recognised his voice. Very distinctive twang. Must have come from Castlewood after us,' Malone replied.

'Oh, I thought the voice was familiar. I've heard him on TV,' Harvey said.

'We need a place for tonight,' Malone said. 'We can try Sandy Trondheim's place. It is somewhere in town…if he hasn't moved.'

'Trondheim? He Norwegian or something?' asked Harvey.

'Yeah, Tryggvi Trondheim. Known as "Sandy" for his reddish-blond hair. Imagines he's a Viking he does. He changed his name from a long Norwegian one, when he settled here, to Trondheim where he was born. I've known him for years. I had forgotten that he had moved to Burton. Now, what was his address? Let me see,' Malone stopped running, sat down on a low wall and searched in the bottom of his knapsack for an old address book.

'Need to look it up quickly, mate, I'm foundered here,' said Harvey as he blew on his hands and did running on the spot to warm himself up.

'Ah, here we are: S.T. 126, Churchyard Lane, Burton. Yep, that's it. I was sure he lived here. Right, let's get over there, and hope he is home,' Malone said as he stood. 'It's not far. There's the church I would guess beyond those trees.' A spire was visible in the distance.

'Okay, lead on.' Harvey yawned loudly. 'Boy, am I tired or what?'

'Me too,' said Malone.

Ten minutes later, Malone rang the doorbell at number 126.

'Who is that at this time of night?' a voice yelled as the owner, Sandy Trondheim, descended the stairs in dressing gown and slippers.

'It's Sid Malone. Is that you, Sandy?' Malone shouted through the letterbox.

Trondheim opened the door. '*For en overrises*! What a surprise. If it isn't Sid Malone! I thought you were locked up or dead long ago, you old scoundrel.'

'Nope, Sandy, very much alive and half-frozen,' Malone laughed.

'Oh, where are my manners? Come in, come in. I'll just turn up the thermostat.' He turned a dial on the wall. 'Who's this lad?' Trondheim asked, looking at Harvey.

'My mate Jake, my partner in crime you might say,' Malone replied. 'We are on the run and need a place to kip for tonight if you can help us.'

'Certainly, certainly, I help you. You can have the back room our boys used. They are away working abroad. A couple of beds just need sheets and stuff. I'll call the wife,' said Trondheim.

'Your wife is here already,' said Mrs Trondheim descending the stairs, hair in curlers. 'Well, well, Sid Malone as I live and breathe. And a handsome young man as well.' She gave each a kiss on the cheek.

'We are sorry to barge in on you like this, Janet, but we are desperate,' Malone said.

'Yes, I heard. Are the cops after the pair of you? There was something on the late news. I just caught the end of it,' Janet laughed. 'Not to worry. Sandy, get bed linen out of the hot-press and make up the beds in our sons' room. We keep a room for them just in case they come home,' she explained. 'I'll get some hot tea into these two waifs. Some food?'

'Yes, please,' said Malone with feeling.

'Yes, my dear,' Trondheim replied and scuttled up the stairs, quite spritely for his sixty-five years. Mrs Trondheim filled the kettle and prepared a pile of sandwiches while it boiled. 'Ham and pickles, do you?' she asked.

'Yes, excellent,' said Malone.

'I will put some soup on for something warming. I'll add a dash of HP sauce for extra zing.' She moved a pot of homemade broth onto the gas.

After they had eaten, Malone and Harvey thanked her profusely. 'That was splendid,' said Malone.

'It certainly was, Mrs Trondheim,' Harvey added.

'Oh, do call me Janet,' she said. She was a local woman who had fallen for Trondheim's charm thirty years ago.

'Right, up to bed then. I've put electric blankets on for you because it's a wintry night,' Sandy Trondheim said.

They all went to bed and soon loud snoring could be heard from the back room.

***

Thursday, February 16th

The sound of traffic in the street wakened the pair eventually. The sun was well risen.

'Oh, sorry, Sandy, we seem to have overslept a little,' said Malone as they came downstairs.

'No problem, guys. The wife has breakfast ready for us. I was just about to waken you,' said Trondheim.

'Yep, I can smell it,' said Harvey, taking a deep, appreciative sniff.

The four of them ate bacon and eggs heartily and then Malone said, 'We should be on our way. We don't want you to be caught for helping us.'

'Nonsense,' said Janet. 'We've been chatting about it, and you can stay as long as you need. It's good to have company. Since our boys moved out of our last house and we came here it has been too quiet by far. There was rarely a quiet minute when they were at home.' She looked sad for a moment and her husband nodded in agreement. 'They were always coming and going to football or the gym or going on dates. Bathroom smelt of aftershave for hours when that happened. Wet socks and shirts though after the football.' She chuckled. 'But they always cleaned their own boots.'

'*Ja*, yes, you must stay longer,' said Trondheim. 'As Janet says we have discussed it and we would love you to stay.'

'Well, how can we refuse, especially after that marvellous breakfast?' said Malone. 'I'm sure the cops will never think of looking here. I hope not anyway.'

'We'll contribute something towards our keep, of course,' said Harvey.

'No, no. Don't worry about that,' said Trondheim. 'We are pleased to help.'

'Thank you so much,' said Harvey, thinking of a good, cooked breakfast every morning.

Trondheim said, 'There was a news bulletin earlier. It said a bank was robbed last night. An undisclosed sum of cash was taken. Would that have been you guys by any chance?'

'Afraid so. We just managed to get away from our hideout, Charlie Jones's place, before the cops raided it. At least I'm sure they suspected it.' The Trondheims looked puzzled. 'It's a long story.' Malone briefly told of the cellar in Jones' house and the cops' visit.

'Sandy, would you mind taking a stroll down to the town centre and see if you can get any news of what the cops are doing?' asked Malone.

'Yes, of course.' Trondheim put on a coat and scarf and taking their pet Rottweiler, Rolf, he set off for a walk.

When he returned about two hours later, he said, 'The gossip is the cops raided a big house but found the birds had flown. The owner and his wife have been held for questioning. I assume that is Charlie and his wife. That's all I could get without sounding too curious, lads.'

'Hmm, that is a pity. We have left the Joneses in trouble,' said Malone.

'I doubt if they could make any charges stick,' said Trondheim. 'A good lawyer will get them off. How were they to know two guests were going to rob a bank?' Jones had managed to conceal his share of the cash before the police returned.

'I hope so,' Harvey said. 'We left no fingerprints, I'm certain.'

They listened to the news every hour that day, and D.I. Denison made a television appeal for help from the public. The photos of the alleged robbers were shown, but the public were warned not to approach "these two dangerous, and probably armed fugitives".

'Hmm, dangerous? I haven't even got a penknife,' said Malone with a chuckle.

'I've just had a brainwave,' Janet Trondheim said. 'We can pass you two off as our sons come home for a long holiday. The neighbours here have never seen them, so for a while, you are Tommy and Kristoffer Trondheim. How does that sound?'

'Sounds brilliant, Janet. Is Tommy the older more handsome one?' Malone asked with a chuckle.

'I don't know about "more handsome", but Tommy is about your age give or take a couple of years, not that folk here would know,' Trondheim replied.

'So, I am Christopher,' said Harvey. 'The really handsome one!'

'Yes, Kristoffer, spelt K-R-I-S-T-O-F-F-E-R.' Janet laughed.

'Right, you must stay indoors for a few days, until things quieten down,' Trondheim said.

'I will go down to the shops later and see what's what,' Janet said. 'I'll try to find out what has happened to the Joneses.'

Trondheim added, 'Shopkeepers always hear all the gossip. If that fails, I'll go to get a haircut. Barbers are a mine of information.' He laughed.

'That's great. Thank you,' Malone said.

'And grow your beards!' Trondheim added. Malone and Harvey stroked their chins and grinned.

Chapter Nineteen

Wednesday, February 22nd

The two robbers had remained in or around the house and had grown a good covering of facial hair. Mrs Trondheim had retrieved some of their sons' old clothes from a storage cupboard. She had intended to bring them to a charity shop, but never got around to it. She always postponed in the hope that the lads would return. The two men managed to find something suitable. The fashion was not too out of date.

'Right,' said Trondheim, 'I think you two are ready to go mobile. I have been telling the neighbours about you and they will be certain you are our lads, so there is no reason others won't be.' He gave each a cover-story of the sons' histories.

Mrs Trondheim added, 'The police seem to have given up the search anyway. I heard that the Castlewood officers have returned to their own place.'

'It is a shame that Charlie and Sarah Jones have been charged with aiding and abetting criminals,' said Malone. 'But the word is Charlie had hidden his loot well, and there are no fingerprints, we wore gloves all the time, so I think they will be acquitted. Can you imagine the court scene?

'My Lord, the defendants are charged with hiding fugitives after a robbery.'

'But, My Lord, no trace of any persons was found on the premises, nor any proceeds of said robbery.'

'Hmm, case dismissed.' They all laughed as Malone strutted around like a lawyer.

'Just had a thought,' said Sandy Trondheim. 'Burton Albion are playing away to Tamworth F.C. in the next round of the National Cup this evening. Why don't we all go since it is local? Make a night of it. A good game of footy, a few bevvies down the Brewer's Arms, some fish and chips. What do you say?'

'Sounds good,' said Harvey. 'We missed the last match as we were otherwise engaged,' he laughed.

'Yes, what's not to like? I'll enjoy that,' Malone said. 'Are you coming, Janet?'

'Just try to stop me! Great Burton fan, I am,' Janet Trondheim replied. 'I must get our football scarves out ready. Better wrap up warm though because it forecasts temperatures near freezing.'

So, just after seven o'clock that evening the four of them piled into the car and drove the twelve miles to Tamworth, a historic market town, and once the capital of the Anglo-Saxon Kingdom of Mercia. Frost sparkled on the lawns and trees as they approached the town.

They drove slowly in a queue up a rough, dusty slope to the club gates. Two stone pillars marked the entrance and a couple of men at a hut were collecting fees for the carpark.

'Plenty of spaces down the far end, mate,' said the collector, Bob Atkins.

Trondheim paid and they drove through the gates.

'Let's go to the little standing-only terrace at the far end. I prefer to stand. It's more fun than sitting. Especially on a frosty night,' Malone suggested.

'Yeah, it's a bit chilly for sitting. Best to be able to move about,' said Trondheim.

Trondheim drove past the turnstiles to the far end of the carpark and pulled into a space.

'Perfect,' said Harvey, getting out of the car. 'Just a perfect spot.' His breath formed a mist as he spoke.

They paid their way in through the last turnstile and headed for the small terrace behind a goal. Iron crush barriers were spaced out along the terrace for spectators to lean on. Most spectators went to the seated areas in the stands. The four fans stood behind a barrier as they watched a number of Burton players warming up and shooting at goal.

Malone groaned. 'Did you see that? Another shot over the bar! What a useless shower! That last one went out of the ground completely! I hope they can do better in the match.' Some of the crowd good-naturedly jeered the player responsible for the ball flying over the fence into trees.

'I think I will get some teas before the kick-off,' said Mrs Trondheim.

'I'll go with you to help carry them,' Malone offered, so the two of them went off in search of refreshments in a pavilion. Harvey and Trondheim stood chatting and reading the match program.

'Three pounds for a program! Daylight robbery. Nothing in it but adverts,' Trondheim complained. 'Oh, here's an advert for cheap lawnmowers! Wish I had a lawn,' he laughed.

Just then, three jolly middle-aged ladies, arms linked, and wearing Burton Albion black and yellow scarves and rosettes, came by merrily singing a football song: "We're on our way to Wembley—" The one in the middle suddenly stopped, bringing them all to a halt.

'Why it's Reverend Matthews, isn't it?' she exclaimed. 'I hardly knew you with that beard.' She looked straight at Harvey. 'And a Burton fan! Good for you.'

'Erm, I think you are mistaken, madam,' Harvey muttered. He spoke in what he hoped was a Norwegian accent. 'Me, a reverend? You have got to be joking. Nah. I am from Norway.'

'Oh, I was sure I recognised you,' said the woman. 'It's me, Edith Pym. Don't you remember me?' Harvey shook his head and looked down at his program.

'Stop bothering the gentleman, Edith,' said one of her companions, and she pulled Edith's arm and they walked on. Edith looked back, still unconvinced that she was wrong. They stopped about fifteen feet away at another crush barrier.

'Edith, did you not hear the news? That man Matthews at the cathedral was an imposter. The real Mr Matthews was found murdered!' said her friend Sadie Turner.

'Yes, that's true,' said the third lady Mrs Turnbull. 'It was awful. The real one, poor man, was discovered in a freezer. Just awful.'

'Oh!' muttered Edith. 'Well, if that was a Norwegian accent, I'm a monkey's auntie. My daughter's married to a Norwegian bloke, and he sounds completely different.'

Meanwhile, the other two returned with four teas.

'A woman just recognised me as Reverend Matthews,' Harvey whispered to Malone.

'Oh, well, I wouldn't worry about it, Jakey. She'll have forgotten about you in ten minutes. Here, drink a cup of tea. Two sugars? It will warm you up.' Harvey sipped the brew.

***

The players came out to start the match to much cheering and waving of scarves. The referee blew the whistle and Burton kicked off.

Tamworth went into the lead with an early penalty, but before long Luke Parker, the new Burton Albion signing, equalised with a volley from fifteen metres. The ball looked like it was going over the bar and the goalkeeper relaxed, but it suddenly dipped behind him and slammed into the back of the net. The Burton fans went wild.

While everyone was watching the match, Edith Pym used her mobile phone to take a video of the crowd including the man she was now completely convinced was the man who impersonated Matthews.

The match ended with a three-one win for Burton: a hat-trick from Parker. The last one kicked from near the centre circle: a real scorcher!

Chapter Twenty

Thursday, February 23rd

Edith Pym had spent a sleepless night. She could not get the encounter at the match out of her head. At seven a.m., she could delay no longer so she dressed, had a quick breakfast and got a taxi to the Burton police headquarters.

'Good morning, madam. How may I assist you?' the sergeant on duty asked. His shift ended in thirty minutes and he hoped this would not take long.

'Well, actually, I may be completely mistaken, but I just need to be sure about something. May I speak to a detective or whoever is in charge of homicide, or whatever you call it?'

'Yes, of course. What homicide is it concerning, may I ask?'

'The murderer of the curate at St John's Cathedral, Castlewood, or to be precise, the impersonator of the curate,' Edith replied.

'Hmm, I see. Please take a seat for a minute and I shall call someone,' said the sergeant indicating a row of plastic seats which had seen better days. A drunk was snoozing in a corner. The sergeant lifted a phone and dialled a number. 'Sergeant Ackroyd here. Could you send a detective out to speak to a lady about the curate George Matthews' murder?'

Minutes later, Detective Sergeant Iain Fitzroy spoke to Edith and led her to an interview room.

'Please take a seat, Mrs Pym. You said you have information concerning the murder of George Matthews,' Fitzroy said.

'Well, I hope so,' said Edith. 'I'm just not sure but I could not sleep for thinking about it.'

'Okay, just tell me what you know,' and he took out a notebook and pencil.

'Last night, two friends and I went to the football, the National Cup match in Tamworth.'

Fitzroy nodded. 'Yes, go on,' he said.

'As we were going along the terrace, the one behind a goal, I noticed a man who looked just like the curate in St John's, or the fake curate as it turns out. He had a beard, but I am certain it was him. It was his eyes mainly: kind of nice but…odd. I cannot explain it. He denied it of course and claimed to be Norwegian, but his accent was fake. There was another man there too. I didn't know him.

'My friend, Sadie, later told me about the real curate's murder. So sad. Anyway, he spoke in a fake Norwegian accent as I've said. I'm certain it was fake. Another man and a woman later joined them.'

'Can you describe them?'

'Hmm, not really. They were all wrapped up in scarves against the cold. Minus four degrees last night, it was,' Edith replied.

'Going to be difficult identifying a man with a beard who could be miles away by now and folk in scarves.'

'Would this help?' said Edith, and she produced her phone and clicked on the video.

'Yes, yes, that is really helpful!' Fitzroy exclaimed. He played the video again. 'There is a good shot of his face, but it will still be difficult to find him.'

Edith took the phone and brought up a photograph. 'Perhaps this will do! As we were leaving the ground, I saw the four of them getting into a red Renault, I think it was, and took a photo of the registration number. I think the badge on the front is Renault.'

Fitzroy positively beamed when he saw the photo. 'Marvellous! You are a wonder, Mrs Pym. This will be an immense help. May I borrow your phone for five minutes until I get these copied?'

'Yes, certainly. Fire away,' Edith smiled and sat back. 'Cuppa tea, two sugars, no milk would be nice,' she added.

Fitzroy laughed. 'Coming right up,' and he left the room. A short time later, a constable brought a cup of tea and a plate of biscuits.

'Thank you very much,' Edith said and grinned. *This will keep me going for a while,* she thought.

'There is a reward if this suspect is convicted, Mrs Pym,' Fitzroy said when he returned the phone.

'Oh, that will be very handy. I'll take my friends on a cruise,' Edith joked. *Or spend it on clothes,* she thought and smiled.

***

Later that day, the detectives from Castlewood arrived back at Burton police H.Q.

'Okay, Iain, what have you got for us?' asked D.I. Denison.

'We have identified an address for the owner of a red Renault,' said Iain Fitzroy, 'believed to be harbouring your criminals Jake Harvey and Sid Malone.' He produced photographs of them attending the football match.

'It certainly could be them if you ignore the face-fuzz. Who is the owner of the car?' asked Denison excitedly, though trying to look calm and unruffled.

'A dodgy character named Tryggvi Trondheim, a Norwegian, of 126, Churchyard Lane, Burton. Trondheim is not his real name. He had it changed when he came over here,' said Fitzroy.

'So, what are we waiting for? Let's go get us a few murderers,' said Denison.

'Harvey and Malone may not be at that address now,' said D.S. Loan, shaking her head.

'I'm just waiting for a search warrant and then we will be off,' D.S. Fitzroy said. Just then, the warrant arrived: an out of breath detective delivered it.

Minutes later, three squad cars sped towards Churchyard Lane. Armed officers were included as Denison thought the suspects might be armed.

D.I. Denison banged on the door of number 126. 'Open up! Police!' he shouted. There was no reply though he could hear movements inside. 'Battering ram,' he shouted to a constable. The man came forward and swung the battering ram against the door. It flew open with the second strike.

The police officers rushed in and caught the two robbers trying to escape through the back door. Four constables blocked their exit.

'Sidney Malone and Jacob Harvey, I arrest you on the suspicion of the murders of Detective Sergeant Gwen Travis,

Detective Constable John Savage, George Matthews, and William Bowler, and for the robbery at the bank in Castlewood. You do not have to say anything, but it may harm your defence if you do not mention something, when questioned, you later rely on in court. Take them away,' Denison said.

Chapter Twenty-One

The two suspects had been left to stew overnight in separate cells. Then Denison began the interviews. He was not in a good mood.

D.S. Fitzroy stated for the recording, 'An interview on 24th February with Sidney Malone, who has declined legal representation. Also present: Detective Inspector Walter Denison and Detective Sergeant Iain Fitzroy.'

Denison sat forward and said, 'Sidney Malone, you are charged with the murders of William Bowler, George Matthews, D.S. Gwen Travis and D.C. John Savage. You are further charged with participating in a bank robbery at the Burton Savings and Investment Bank Ltd. on Wednesday the fifteenth of February. What have you to say to the charges?' Denison sat back in his chair and stared at Malone.

Malone sat for a moment before he spoke. 'Where's your proof, copper? I have not killed any of those people, and I didn't do any bank job.' He sneered. 'At least not for years,' he grinned.

Denison resumed. 'You and Harvey attacked and drowned...' Malone raised an eyebrow. 'Yes, drowned. The two police officers you attacked in Edward Street were still alive when you threw them into the river. You also butchered Billy Bowler in a most heinous way and murdered or assisted Harvey by murdering and him impersonating the curate, George Matthews.'

'I had nothing to do with them there murders. Maybe Harvey did, I don't know. I knew he wasn't really a clergyman. I thought he was just having a laugh. He was always wanting to be an actor, but I never knew about no murder. I thought he was just mucking about pretending to be working in the cathedral. Just a bit of a lark, as a cover, like.'

'We have the two weapons used on the two officers. Covered in your DNA and prints, Malone.'

'I don't believe you,' Malone sneered. 'Couldn't be.'

'Why not? Because you chucked them in the river after you drowned the officers? Denison said firmly.'

'Them clubs—' Malone bit his tongue, realising he had said too much.

'Yes, Malone, the golf clubs you and Harvey used.'

'It…it is common knowledge out there.' Malone gestured towards the window. 'Everyone is saying they were hit with golf clubs.'

'They have been matched by pathology to the injuries on the victims. A number of hairs, which should match your DNA I'm thinking, were found by forensics on Billy Bowler's remains. I am sure Harvey will confirm you were up to your neck in the murder of Matthews, too,' Denison said firmly. 'Lock him up, Iain. I would advise you to get a good lawyer, Malone. You are going to need one.'

'No comment,' Malone smirked.

***

D.I. Denison stated for the recording, 'An interview with Jacob Lee Harvey, his legal representative Harry Grimley. Also present: Detective Sergeant Iain Fitzroy and me, Detective Inspector Walter Denison.'

Harvey was quaking in his trainers but tried to look smug. 'I ain't done nothing, Denison. I am absolutely innocent.'

'Perhaps you are, perhaps you are not. Mr Malone has told us his version,' Denison said. He let that sink in before continuing, 'And it does not bode well for you, Mr Harvey. Not well at all!'

'Why? What has he said?' Harvey sat forward, looking worried.

D.S. Iain Fitzroy said, 'We shall come to that in due course. Where did you get the idea of taking George Matthews place as curate? You cannot really deny that is what you did.'

'You do not need to answer that,' said the lawyer.

'I'll admit I took Matthews' place, but it was Malone who did him in. Malone killed him, I swear,' Harvey almost shouted as he tried to put the blame on Malone. 'He only told me later that he was dead, and that I should take his place. He had all the letters and stuff, which had been sent to Matthews. I had to go along with it because he is vicious. Nothing I could do about it, so I turned up for the job just before Christmas, as I needed a place to hide. The cops in Manchester were after me for burglaries, which I did not do, I hasten to add. I was planning on skedaddling after a few weeks.'

'How about the murder of our two colleagues? The golf clubs with your prints all over them…' Denison changed tack suddenly.

'Couldn't be! Malone chucked them in the riv…' Too late, Harvey stopped his lips flapping, but Denison leaned forward and smiled in Harvey's face.

'Malone implied you chucked them after you killed the two officers,' Denison exaggerated slightly.

'No! No, he's not putting the blame on me. He killed them when I was getting in my car. It took a while to start it. He made me help him throw them in the river. That's the truth.'

'Now, to return to the student. Who killed him?' Denison asked.

'I'll tell you the whole story if I get a reduced sentence and a prison far away from Malone. He'd kill me the first chance he got!'

'I cannot promise a reduced sentence,' said Denison, 'but I shall mention your co-operation to the judge. I will also make sure you are locked up in a separate nick from Malone.' *If I can that is,* Denison thought to himself.

'Right, well, as I said,' Harvey began as he sat back in his chair wringing his hands and perspiring profusely, 'we were on the run from Manchester's cops, and a few members of other gangs, too. Malone owed them thousands of pounds. Malone saw the student guy and could see he was like my twin, so he got chatting with him in a café. Pally, he was. He found out this guy, the real George Matthews, was going to do a spot of curating in the cathedral so he followed him to his digs at the Theo-what's-it college.'

'Theological College?' Denison suggested helpfully.

Harvey nodded. 'It was Malone, not me, what done him in. Malone got the idea of me imper…impro…'

'Impersonating?' Denison suggested.

'Yeah that. Well, if I had a cosy job like, Malone thought, then he could share my digs somewhere around the cathedral. Only as it turned out my room was too small for two and my landlady said that it broke fire regulations or something, and everything at the cathedral was locked up like Fort Knox, so he got a room elsewhere.

'Anyway, before he killed the student, he phoned me and told me to come to the guy's, Matthews' flat, and I took some of his clothes, books, papers, the letter of appointment and stuff. I took from the letter that the staff had never met Matthews, so we were flying. My face was close enough to Matthews' driving licence photo to be twins. Malone put the kid in an old freezer and turned it on, and we left. Malone killed him.

'All went well, except I made a few, well, a lot of silly mistakes so I would probably have been fired before long. And then I got a text one morning saying you guys had sussed that I was fake because the body had been found.'

'Who texted you?' Denison demanded to know.

'Don't know,' said Harvey.

Denison looked sceptical. 'Do you expect us to believe that?'

'I swear I don't. It was just from "A Friend", a friend of Malone's I suppose. Malone never said who his informant was. I just got texts, or he got texts, unsigned.'

'He never gave any clue about this person's identity?' Fitzroy asked. 'A name, male or female?'

'He let slip once, now you ask, that their name began with an *S*. I supposed it was a name anyway. Could be a nickname or something. I assumed he, or she, was a copper because they knew what you guys were doing. Knew your every move. Had to be on the inside. Malone said it was better that I did not know the name. "What you don't know you cannot blab" kind of idea.' Harvey was sweating profusely by this time.

'Did you kill Billy Bowler?' Denison asked, abruptly changing the subject.

Harvey sat forward. 'No! I certainly did not! No, that was all Malone's doing. Malone was told by some friends of his that Billy had been seen with some of your lot and was blabbing. We both went to see him at his digs. I thought it was just to scare him into silence, but he and Malone started arguing. Billy threw a punch and before I knew what was happening, Malone drew a knife from his belt and held it to Billy's throat. Malone had gone crazy, I tell you. Billy was forced down on the bed screaming for mercy, and Malone told me, no, ordered me to tie him up; he was waving the knife around. I used Billy's shirts. I tore off the sleeves and used those. I was scared Malone would do me too if I refused. I had never seen him so…furious. Yeah, furious is the word. Malone then carved something on Billy's chest with the knife. I did not see what 'cause I had backed over to the door. I was ready to run but felt paralysed and couldn't move. I was really scared, me! I almost threw up because there was blood everywhere. I hate the sight o' blood.

'Malone then…' Harvey swallowed hard as beads of sweat trickled down his brow, 'then he began cutting him. There was even more blood. Billy was screaming something awful, and Malone stuffed something in his mouth to gag him. It just seemed to go on and on.' Harvey began trembling. 'Eventually, I could stand it no longer and ran out of the house. I ran for miles, it seemed like. Then I eventually, after a couple of hours, went back to his hideout. Malone was just so calm like nothing had happened at all. I and been scared he might turn on me. I was still shaking like a leaf. I never spoke about that day again until now. That's the truth, Inspector,' Harvey concluded.

'So, you are saying that Malone did all four killings? You are just an innocent forced to participate?' Denison said with heavy sarcasm. 'Interview suspended.'

Chapter Twenty-Two

Next morning, Saturday, February 25th

Denison called the team together in his office. 'As we could have predicted, both suspects are blaming each other for the murders.' He did not mention the *S* name. He told Fitzroy to keep it under his hat. 'I am leaving them for today to stew a while and will interview them again tomorrow or Monday. Okay, carry on, troops.' Everyone stood and went about their duties.

Denison decided to take the rest of the weekend off. He wanted time to think, so he murmured that he "did not feel too good" and went home to Castlewood.

He and his wife lived in a modest detached house in the northern suburb. Their two children, aged eleven and thirteen, were in boarding school. The parents believed in getting the best education possible.

'Do you want some lunch, Dearest?' his wife, Millicent, shouted from the kitchen.

'Not very hungry at the moment, Dear. Leave a plate of sandwiches for later, please. I'll eat them when I feel the worms calling,' he joked.

'Yes, okay. I'll have a quick salad myself and leave ham and salad sandwiches. Then I am off to visit poor Mrs Travers.

She's not so well, poor woman. Her back is bad again and she can hardly move.'

'Very well, Dear,' replied Denison and he sat in his favourite well-worn armchair by the open fire in the living room and produced his pipe. He put his feet up on a footstool.

'Don't you dare be thinking of smoking that smelly thing in the house, or I'll knock your pan in, Walter Denison!' his wife exclaimed from the hallway, hands on hips and a glare on her face.

'I'm not lighting it. It…it just helps me think things through. It worked for Sherlock. Got a tough problem to work on, Dearest.'

'Hmm, that's all right then, but he is fictional, remember,' and she put on a coat and a hat. She always, but always, wore a hat when out in public, like the queen. 'One may be on one's uppers, but one can still look dignified,' she often explained. Not that the Denisons were "on their uppers" but it pleased her. *Anything for a quiet life,* her husband always thought.

As soon as she left, Denison counted slowly to twenty, in case of a return, then opened a window and lit up. He pulled his chair closer but found the chilly breeze too much, so he reluctantly tapped the pipe out and closed the window again. *Roll on summer,* he thought with a smile.

'Now, where to start?' he muttered to himself as he settled down comfortably by the fire. He removed his waistcoat and tie. Not that the waistcoat fitted around him anyway. 'Superintendent Harris noted, "Why was the fake curate, only texted a warning a matter of minutes before you arrived? No, the culprit must be here," in Castlewood that is. Manchester would have warned him ages before,' Denison shuddered. 'Someone connected with the case, especially with a name or nickname beginning with an *S*. And I really must stop talking to myself, Cedric,' he laughed. 'Still, at least if I am talking to myself, it is to someone sensible! If you are going to talk to someone, Cedric, make it to a genius.'

Cedric opened an eye, stretched a leg, licked a paw briefly and curled up once more in front of the open fire. He was a large tabby and white tomcat whose main aim in life was to sleep and eat as much as possible. He occasionally deigned to patrol the garden just in case any other cats dared to invade his territory.

Denison resumed his soliloquy. 'First, I can discount myself, unless I'm a sort of Jekyll and Hyde character,' Denison chuckled. 'Then we have Mary Loan, Emily Young, Sam Potter, Sean-Patrick Kelly, Sandra Johnston. Oh, and Sol Reid from the other part of the office.' He underlined the *S*s as he printed the names on a pad. 'Six suspects.'

'Cannot really see Sol Reid being close enough to the action to inform the baddies. He sits away at the other end of the main office and couldn't hear what goes on in my room, not with the glass partition and him hard of hearing. He has seemed a little quiet recently, I noticed. Not his usual cheerful self. Personal problems perhaps. Anyway, he works for D.I. Cranford in "Narcotics", so has no connection to our squad. From Stratford-upon-Avon though, if I recall correctly.' He jotted down Stratford-u-A on his pad underlining the *S*. 'Hmm, I wonder if the *S* could be a place. That is a tenuous connection, but I'll check the others too. Mary did say none were from Manchester. Besides, Sol, was quick enough to help with the canal boat.' Denison's thoughts came fast and furiously. 'He could have denied knowing the sound of the boat had he been protecting Malone and Harvey. Okay,

Walter, put Sol to the bottom of the pile, at least for the moment.' He put a number six beside Sol's name.

'Hmm, I do feel peckish now. I think I'll have a bite to eat, and I really must stop talking to myself,' he laughed. He went into the kitchen followed by Cedric who thought food might be on offer. Denison consumed all that his wife had prepared then opened a tin of rice pudding with peaches. He was partial to peaches.

Cedric miaowed hopefully and sat with his head cocked to one side.

'Hmm, that will do me for a while,' said Denison. He dabbed his mouth with a napkin. 'I suppose you want fed too, cat.' Denison opened a tin of "Kit-E-Kat Tuna and Salmon" and put the contents in the cat's bowl. Cedric sniffed the food, seemed to find it acceptable then started eating. Denison smiled and said, 'Enjoy. You cats can be very fussy eaters. I remember we tried you on cheaper brands and you turned your nose up at them. Oh well, it's back to the grindstone for me, old chap.'

He switched on his laptop and brought up staff records. 'Mary has already searched these but won't do any harm to double-check.' He entered the names of the team and searched "Manchester connection". 'Hmm, no connection at all with anyone. But one of them must have a connection with the pair of criminals. Wait a second. Mary is from Salford, Manchester! She never mentioned that. But the leak must be here in Castlewood. It is certainly not at the Manchester end. Of that, I am certain.' He wrote down Salford.

'Emily Young? No *S* in her name though. Middle name's Jennifer. She seemed really keen to track them down, especially after she got the email about the body found in the freezer. Born in S̲t Helens though. That is well away from Manchester.' Again, he underlined the *S* as he jotted down the details.

'Oh, just remembered, who was it came through the office when Emily got the email about the body found in the freezer? Emily was very enthusiastic, I recall, so I think I can set her name to one side.' He put a five next to her name.

He thought for several moments. 'Yes, it was the pathologist, S̲amantha Nixon. Another *S*!' He printed her name, underlined the *S*, and checked her record for a Manchester connection. 'Hmm, she lived there until five years ago, in S̲tretford, Manchester. That's interesting. So, assuming she saw the email she could have texted Harvey and he scarpered from the cathedral pronto. Not proof, but it fits. And she came into the room that time we were talking about Matthews' digs. She could have warned Harvey to be careful. Hmm, so we now have seven suspects. Right, Walter, put her at the top of the list of suspects.' He amended the numbers on the previous two to seven and six. 'I wonder…I wonder if young Wartonberry could do a check on her phone without her knowing. Hmm.' He tapped the pen on the notepad and smiled with satisfaction. 'What do you think, Cedric old chap?' Cedric, his stomach full and feeling quite comfortable in front of the fire, opened an eye lazily but detecting no sign of more food or a tummy rub, he closed the eye again. The tip of his tail flicked a few times, and he went back to sleep.

'Hmm, a fat lot of help you are. If I opened some more cat food, you would be more interested, eh?' Denison chuckled. 'Right, who's next? S̲andra? I remember her seeming to be shocked that a police officer could be tipping off the criminals. Oh, and she was over the moon when her informer said that the pair had moved to Burton: "One of my snitches has told me that Malone and Harvey have moved to Burton." Born in, let's see, S̲toke-on-Trent. A local girl. No Manchester connection. I think I can strike Sandra off the suspects too, so number five on the list. For the moment, at least.'

'S̲am Potter? On the face of it, he is too guileless to be a good deceiver. Or is he a good actor? Nah, he is all copper down to his bootlaces, is Potter. Besides, he was eager to get Bowler as an informant. He would not have been keen were he in league with Malone and Harvey. Born in S̲heffield though. Why is everyone born in a place with an *S*? Coincidence? It must be! Do I believe in coincidences?

'Brr! Getting chilly in here!' He reached for a log from a basket and threw it on the fire. The cat awoke, stretched and curled up again. 'Ever so sorry for disturbing you, Your Majesty,' Denison smiled.

'Now, where was I? Sam Potter. Sam was the one who saw the resemblance between Matthews and Harvey. He would not have been surprised had he known the gang. So, strike Sam for the moment, too. Sam, number four. Hmm, progress. Besides, he had moved from Sheffield to Colchester before he came here.'

'What about S̲ean-Pat Kelly? He took it really badly when we searched their phones. Of course, that could be a natural reaction, or he was scared something might be found. Ah, born in S̲words. That's near Dublin if I remember correctly. I think I will put him as the number two suspect. Oh, just a thought: he pronounces Sean as **Sh**aun so not really an S sound. That could let him off the hook. Number five then.' He amended the others accordingly.

Just then, he heard the front door opening. 'Hi, I'm home, husband dear,' his wife called.

'The present Mrs Denison has returned, Cedric,' he said softly, then louder, 'You're home early, Mrs Denison number one. I thought you were going to visit poor Mrs Travers,' Denison replied. His little joke was to pretend he could divorce his beloved and marry another. His missus knew better. Her hubby would give up his pipe before he gave her up.

'I did, but then her son, his stuck-up wife and four kids arrived. Four little horrors. I made my excuses and left. I cannot abide those kids. So ill-mannered! If I were their mother, they would all be in boarding school…in Australia! Can't abide her either. All airs and graces, lah-de-dah!'

'You ate the sandwiches, I see,' she said as she entered the kitchen.

'Yes, I felt a little peckish after a while. Thinking is demanding work,' he laughed.

'And a whole tin of rice pudding…and peaches!' She rinsed and threw the tins in the recycling bin. 'Do you want anything more now?'

'Cup of coffee would go down a treat, Dearest.'

'Okay, I'll put the kettle on.'

'And some of that chocolate cake!' Denison added. 'A big slice.'

Where does he put it all? she thought. *I'm not mending those trousers again. He'll have to buy a new suit whether he likes it or not.* 'You'll have to buy a new suit. I am not mending that one again!'

'Anything you say, Dear,' he replied. 'Pigs might fly, Cedric,' he whispered.

When he had eaten, Denison returned to his laptop. His missus went upstairs for a nap.

He resumed his musings again. 'Which only leaves Nixon and Mary Loan. When we had a location at Trondheim's place, Mary was quick to say: "Harvey and Malone may not be at that address now." And when we were going to speak to the curate, fake curate, she needed to nip to the "ladies". And when we spoke to the staff at the cathedral, she blamed the Manchester Met. for the leak: "That means there is a leak in Manchester Met's C.I.D." I wonder, was this to divert attention from herself?

'When Malone had escaped from the flat in Castlewood, she said it looked like the gang had been warned: "Looks like he was warned that we had an address. If only we knew who told him," so why would she say that if she were the informer? Hmm, because she had nothing to hide, or because she wished to divert attention? Hmm, it is difficult to imagine her betraying her colleagues…and me! How long have we worked together, Cedric? Years!

'Also, on her credit side, she was worried about the effect on the team to have the phones checked: "But just suppose none of them is guilty, it will destroy the team's morale." Though, I did speak to her about setting the trap at their new hideout with Manchester. And she was insistent that the leak was there: "The leak must be in Manchester," she said. But then again, they were not warned straight away to scarper. She could have texted them straight away, or was she afraid that would point the finger at her? She did look extremely disappointed when the phone check drew a blank. Drat, I'm going around in circles here!' He scratched his head, stretched and yawned. Cedric stretched and yawned too.

'Then again, she was quick to implicate Nixon: "Could it be Samantha Nixon?" she asked. And there is the fact she never said that she was from Salford! A Manchester connection. Could the *S* really be a place, and not a person's name, or even *S* for sergeant, or perish the thought, superintendent? Doesn't sound likely. Okay, Mary as the number two suspect, reluctantly, which leaves Samantha Nixon as my number one suspect. I'll have another chat with Malone and see if I can clarify things. I will have to try to trick him into revealing something. I don't believe Harvey knows who the informant is. Not too bright is that lad.'

Denison wrote down his finalised list of suspects: Samantha, Mary, Sam, Sandra, Emily, Sean and Sol. He hesitated and then crossed off Sean and Sol's names as being unlikely.

He turned off the laptop, put it to one side, sat back and began to doze. Cedric, on cue, stretched, jumped onto Denison's lap and made himself comfortable. A paw rubbed on Denison's cheek. 'You're good to yourself, aren't you, Cat?' he murmured and scratched a feline ear.

Loud purring ensued.

Chapter Twenty-Three

Monday, February 27ᵗʰ

D.I. Denison decided to try another interview with Malone and returned to Burton-upon-Trent. D.S. Fitzroy was warned not to react to anything which Denison said.

'Have you decided to own up and admit all the murders, Malone?' Denison asked.

'Nope. I am as innocent as a totally innocent newborn babe,' Malone smirked and laughed at his own joke.

'Who is "S"? Give me a name.'

'Ha, where did you get that from? Has that got you worried, copper?' replied Malone.

'Harvey said that you were being informed by a person whose name begins with an *S*. I want to know who it is. It may not make any difference to your sentence, but it will be a mark in your favour,' said Denison. 'Or maybe the *S* is just a decoy. Perhaps the *S* is not a name…' Denison noticed a twitch on Malone's face. 'Does *S* refer to a place?'

'A place? It might, or on the other hand, it might not,' Malone grinned. 'If I knew what you are talking about, of course.' Denison felt that he was on the right track.

'So, let's say it is a place, a code word for someone, for the sake of argument. Is it in Manchester?' Denison asked.

Malone began to wonder how much he knew. 'Just supposing, for the sake of argument, I told you and you caught your mole, alleged mole, what's in it for me? You scratch my back and maybe I'll scratch yours.' Malone grinned.

'Might go in your favour with the judge for a few years off your sentence. We have enough forensic evidence to convict you for four murders. The only question is how many years you wish to serve.'

Malone jumped up, 'I am not taking the rap for the student's murder. That was Jake Harvey, not me. I had nothing to do with it.'

'Sit down!' Denison said firmly. 'So, are you admitting the other murders?'

Malone thought for a moment, to control his emotions. 'Of course not. I am just denying the student's murder.

'I cannot, being a man of honour, come right out and give you a name, Inspector. Goes against the grain somewhat.' He grinned. 'That would be grassing as we, shall we say, in the law-breaking class would say.'

'Does the name "Salford" mean anything to you?'

Malone raised an eyebrow. 'Er, Salford? Why should it? It is part of Greater Manchester, that's all.'

'It is where your informant comes from, if I am not mistaken, Malone. I just need a nod from you,' Denison said and leaned forward. 'Time off your sentence!'

Again, Malone said, 'That would be grassing. You will have to do better than that, copper.'

'Interview ended,' Denison said. Denison was inwardly seething. So near yet so far away.

***

'Iain, I am convinced Salford is the code for the informer. One of those who work in Castlewood, I'm afraid,' said Denison to Fitzroy.

'I have the feeling you are right, sir. But who is it and how can we go about getting proof?' replied D.S. Fitzroy.

'I don't know, yet. If I confront this person, they will just deny it and all their phones have already been checked. Wartonberry, our tech guy, said Samantha Nixon's phone is clean. She's my main suspect and our pathologist by the way.' He did not mention D.S. Loan's connection with Salford. He could not bring himself to believe that it was her.

'How about a pay-as-you-go phone, sir? The suspect could have one and used it to inform the gang,' suggested Fitzroy.

'Yes, quite likely. It would be the easiest way, but I feel reluctant to act without proof. Might just have to bite the bullet and get a search warrant for the suspect's home and locker at the station.'

Denison drove home and wondered what the best course of action was.

'You are going to upset your detectives no matter what you do, Dear, so just confront the situation,' his wife advised that evening. Denison had outlined his dilemma.

'Yes, I will have to. I'll get the lot of them in my office and tell them I am going to have them all investigated. The guilty party will, hopefully, confess or be found out. Yes, that's the solution. Thank you, my dear. Now, whose turn is it to make the cocoa?'

'Yours, of course,' his wife replied without hesitation.

'Hmm, it is always my turn,' he grunted. 'Ham sandwich?'

'Yes, please but no mustard, Dear,' she said. 'It'll keep me awake half the night.'

'Ham sans mustard it is.'

Chapter Twenty-Four

The next morning, February 28th

The four detective constables, plus D.S. Loan and Samantha Nixon were called into Denison's office. The two men leaned against the wall, and the women sat at each end of Denison's desk. The door to the main office was closed. The officers there were curious as to what was happening. They sensed something was in the wind.

'There is no easy way to say this, so here goes. I have concluded, reluctantly, that the informer is one of you six,' said Denison. There were immediate protests.

'We have been through all that, sir,' said Sandra Johnston.

'And nothing was found, sir, nothing!' added Sam Potter. The others muttered agreement.

'I know, but the fact remains that one of you has been in league with Malone and Harvey. Therefore, as I speak, a task force is searching your homes and lockers here for a secret phone.'

'I don't believe this! You are searching...' D.C. Emily Young began.

'Searching our homes? You have ordered a search. Dis is too much. I want our Union rep. here. Dis is unbelievable,' Sean-Pat Kelly protested.

Denison almost shouted, 'I remind you to show respect, Detective.'

A knock came to the door into the corridor. 'Enter!' Denison said sharply.

A uniformed sergeant, Cyril Benson, came in and Denison asked, 'Well, did you find anything?'

'No, sir, nothing. Clean as a whistle,' the sergeant replied.

'Search their desks out there—' Denison halted mid-sentence. In a normal voice, he continued, 'Sol, could you come in here a minute, please?' He had caught sight of D.C. Sol Reid at the far end of the main office watching intently. Reid visibly jumped and after hesitating, stood and walked towards Denison's office. 'Open the door please, Sean-Pat,' Denison said. D.C. Kelly did so, and Reid entered. His face was pale. The six others and Sergeant Benson looked mystified.

'Well, now, Sol,' Denison began, 'you seem to have been following proceedings in here rather intently, have you not?'

'Erm, no, sir,' Reid muttered. 'I, er, just noticed something was going on, sir.'

'You wear a hearing aid, don't you, Sol?'

'Yes, sir, in my right ear, sir. Deaf as a post in my left. Which is why I am on office duties, mainly,' said Reid.

'And therefore, Detective, I am led to the conclusion that you can lip-read. Am I right?' Denison glowered at him.

'Er, yes, a little, sir.' Reid cringed.

'And I also conclude that you quite possibly have been lip-reading what has been going on in here as regards Malone and Harvey these past few weeks. Am I right?' Denison stood and leaned forward, hands on his desk. The others looked on mouths agape. They had no idea what was happening.

Sol Reid quailed and went even paler. 'No, no, sir, definitely not, sir.'

'I had put you down as impossible to be involved, Reid, until you seemed so interested just now. Perhaps I was mistaken. I wonder if we were to search your desk…'

'You cannot do that! It's…it's private, that is,' Reid protested. His face was deathly pale.

'Sergeant Benson will you and D.C. Kelly go and search this person's desk?' Denison ordered.

The two men went up the main office to Reid's desk and did so. With a finger and thumb, Kelly lifted an object from the bottom drawer. 'Would dis be what you were lookin' for, sorr?' Denison and the others had followed them up the office.

Denison took the proffered phone and switched it on. He pressed "messages" and a number of texts were revealed. 'You did not even have the wit to delete this stuff, Reid. I quote: "They know you not real curate. Denison on way. Get out," end quote. Dated 18 January.' The others stood open-mouthed.

D.S. Loan said, 'The date we went to catch the fake curate!'

'Exactly,' Denison said.

'You mean to say that Sol has been informing them all along, sir?' Mary Loan asked.

'That is exactly what I mean. The question is why. What have you to tell us, Reid? And it had better be good.'

Sol Reid visibly wilted and grabbed the desk for support. He sat down and put his head in his hands. 'I'm sorry. I'm sorry,' he exclaimed. 'I had to do what Malone said. He has my sister hidden away somewhere. She's only seventeen. I don't know who is holding her or where, but I was allowed to speak to her only once on the phone. Malone said that she would be safe as long as I did what I was told. There is only me and her, no other family, which is why her kidnapping was never reported. She was not working or studying so no one missed her.' The detectives looked at each other.

Emily Young was the first to speak. 'Which means she is still a captive…somewhere.'

'YES! If she is still alive,' Reid almost screamed. He looked from face to face helplessly. Tears rolled down his face.

'Right, get Malone into the interview room, now,' Denison said. 'Put Reid in my office and guard him for the moment, Sean. I'll deal with him later.'

'By the way, I never knew you were from Salford, Mary,' said Denison.

'Oh, yes, I am, sir. There are a lot of Marys in our family: Aunt Mary from Birmingham, "Brum Mary"; Great Aunt Mary from Leicester, "Leicester Mary"; Aunt Mary from Leeds, "Leeds Mary"; and me, "Salford Mary" from Salford.' Everyone laughed. 'We used the nicknames so we would know which of us was being spoken of.'

Denison chuckled. 'Okay, Salford Mary, come with me to the interview room.'

'Right then, Malone, no more fooling about,' said Denison. 'We know about Reid and you having his sister kidnapped. Where is she? Tell us NOW!' Denison wished he could resort to thumping the prisoner.

Malone squirmed but only said, 'No comment.'

'Tell us where. She had better be unharmed or you will spend the rest of your life behind bars. I'll see that you do.'

'So! As I am charged with multiple homicides already another one won't matter,' Malone grinned. He was putting on a show of bravado.

'She is an innocent caught up in your twisted life. Her family must be frantic.' Malone did not know Sol was her only relative.

Malone said, 'Okay, what does it matter? I'll tell you **if** it goes in my favour.'

'I'll see that it is mentioned to the judge,' Denison said.

Malone nodded. 'She is in a flat at 21A, Port Madoc Drive, Manchester. I'm sure she is still okay. I told our bloke to do nothing until he heard from me.'

The Manchester police were contacted and an hour later, the girl was reported safe and well, if very hungry and dishevelled. The man, Ralph Mulholland, guarding her had fled when he heard Malone had been arrested, but was tracked down in a few days and was arrested. His fingerprints were all over the room where the girl had been held prisoner.

***

'Well, Denison, that was excellent work,' said Chief Superintendent Harris in Castlewood. 'All the gang under lock and key, and the kidnap victim safe, thankfully.

'I am, however, devastated that one of our own officers was assisting the gang. This must never happen again. Never. The newspapers are making the most of this betrayal, so Reid must be put on trial, soon as.'

Denison replied, 'I totally agree, sir, but given the circumstances who of us can say that we would not have done the same? It is a dilemma I hope I never have to face.'

'Hmm, true enough but justice must take its course. Anyway, the gang will be locked away for many years so that is one good result. Now, you and your officers deserve a reward.'

'That won't be necessary, sir. All part of the job,' said Denison.

'Nevertheless, I think three days paid leave is on the cards. Just keep it between us, eh?' said the superintendent. 'We'll put you all down as being on a training course somewhere.'

'Certainly, sir, we'll keep schtum. All the rest would be wanting leave too,' Denison chuckled. 'I'll go and break the good news to the troops. I think I'll treat the missus to a trip to Wales to visit her relatives. Snowdon is nice at this time of year.'

'Very good, off you go,' said Harris and he smiled. He knew Mrs Denison loved Wales. The cat would, of course, go too.

II
The Informers' Murders

Chapter One

To say Detective Chief Inspector Denison, recently promoted, was as broad as he was tall might be an exaggeration, but only a slight one. Aged forty-five, he stood five feet five inches in his socks and still had a large waistline. His trousers' waistband had received several inserts sewn by his devoted wife, Millicent. When it had come to the choice between getting a larger car and going on a diet, Denison had shunned the diet option.

***

'Well, Cedric, now the lady of the house has departed on a shopping expedition with my money, I shall indulge in a pipe or two. Don't you even think of telling her.' Denison smiled to himself.

Cedric was a large tabby and white cat curled up on a rug in front of the open fire. His favourite spot. He opened an eye and blinked twice then went back to sleep.

Denison opened a window because Mrs D. detested pipe smoke.

'Confound the man!' he exclaimed when he opened the window, 'Why can't he muck-spread when it's raining?'

Denison spoke of the farmer he nicknamed "Old McDonald" after the children's song character. He did not know his real name. (McPain-in-the-neck or something, he always said). 'Every day it is sunny at this time of year, there he is happily spreading misery to all and sundry. I'm convinced he deliberately waits till the wind is in this direction. Confound the man!' The unbearable stench was unavoidable.

Denison closed the window and resorted to setting his bulk down on the rug beside the cat so his pipe smoke would ascend the chimney. 'Ah, that's better,' he sighed. 'And don't look at me like that, Cat, you don't own this rug and you have had your breakfast so be grateful; you could be dumped off at a Dogs' Home, so be warned.' Cedric went back to sleep.

'Great to have a few days off work,' Denison sighed happily. 'Nothing to do and all day to do it in,' he grinned. 'I really must stop talking to myself.

'If anyone dares to phone, I shall tell them where to go in no uncertain terms, that's for sure.'

Five minutes later, the telephone rang! 'NO! NO!' Denison yelled at it. 'Shut up! Go away!' It did neither.

Reluctantly, he got up with difficulty and shambled over to the phone. 'Yes, who is this?' he barked, ready to chew someone's head off.

'Superintendent Harris here, Denison,' the reply came. This was the Chief Superintendent of Castlewood Police, John Harris.

'Oh, good morning, sir.' Denison was suddenly very polite.

'Sorry to disturb you on your day off, Denison, but something has come up.'

Denison suddenly had a foreboding of great magnitude. 'Oh, what, sir?'

'A veritable massacre is the only way to describe it. Six men, some of whom at least have assisted us in the past, informers you understand, have been found tortured and shot. They are in a house on the edge of town. Shocking scene I'm told, shocking. Blood everywhere.'

***

Castlewood, a small city in Staffordshire, England, had been the scene of the search for two murderers, Malone and Harvey, some five years before. Denison had led the team which put them behind bars.

Most of the team were still with promoted D.C.I. Denison: Detective Constables Emily Young and Samuel Potter, Detective Sergeant Sandra Johnston with Detective Inspector Mary Loan. Only D.C. Sean-Patrick Kelly had moved to a new post in the London Metropolitan Police. Other officers were also involved as befitted Denison's new rank.

Chapter Two

'Well, so much for a peaceful day off, Cedric. I have to go to work. You wouldn't know the meaning of the word, being a cat. They talk of a dog's life being good. Ah well,' he sighed as he put on a jacket, and gave his hair, what was left of it, a quick comb. 'Better leave a note for the missus, I suppose.' He wrote a brief note and propped it up on the hall table as he departed.

At the crime scene, a forensic officer, Charlie Goldson, gave a brief description of the apparent events: 'Six bodies, sir, all male. They appear to have suffered prolonged torture followed by a bullet in the head or strangled in one case. I assume a silencer was used. One of your colleagues has identified one of the dead. Oh, here she comes now.' D.S. Johnston came out of the house wearing white overalls.

'Good morning, sir,' she said. 'Sorry for dragging you out on your day off.'

'Not a problem. Who wants days off anyway?' Denison grinned. 'Our friend here,' he indicated the forensic officer, 'says you identified one body.'

'Yes, sir, it's Wally Mulgrew, what's left of him, poor blighter. It was him who told me where Malone and Harvey were hiding out, if you remember, a few years ago?'

'Yes, very well. Difficult to forget that pair. So, do you think there may be a connection?' Denison asked.

Johnston replied, 'Possibly, but as those two are still locked up for many years to come it might be jumping to conclusions. But Sam Potter says he thinks that some of the other victims were snitches in the Malone case too. Hard to be certain considering their, erm, condition.'

'Hmm,' Denison mused. 'Well, I had better take a look.' He put on the largest overalls available and went into the house.

The scene shocked even him for all his experience with murder cases: every wall was splattered with blood. Two mutilated, partially clothed bodies lay in the living room, one in the hallway, and three upstairs in a bedroom.

Denison felt he was ready to be sick after touring the premises but took a deep breath. 'Which one is Mulgrew?'

'The one by the window in the living room, sir,' Johnston replied. Denison moved carefully over to the body. "Remains" might have been a more suitable description. All the fingers had been cut off, ears likewise. Some skin had been peeled from the torso and hung in bloody strips from the waist. 'The dismembered digits, a few toes, and the ears of all six are over there in that bucket, sir. The gang have been very "tidy" in that respect. I say gang because I doubt if one person could have done this.'

Denison felt queasy. 'I'll…I'll take a look later, Sandra.

'Right, we will let forensics continue and the coroner remove the bodies to the pathology lab. We will set about identifying the rest and checking for a Malone/Harvey connection. Okay, let's go,' and the detectives all left the house.

***

Some hours later

'Right, what have we found out about the six victims? Are they connected in any way, apart from being dead?' Denison asked his squad assembled in his office. His new office was allocated when he was promoted, which was about five square metres larger than his old one.

Detective Inspector Mary Loan produced a file and read, 'Sir, the victims are all local men. These are their names: Walter "Wally" Mulgrew, David Markovich, Thomas Speers, Ivor Williams, Benjamin Bancroft and Eli Leonard.

'Speers could only be identified by a tattoo on his forearm. His teeth had been knocked out.' She handed out copies of the list to each of the team. 'So far we have established that they were **all** involved as informers when we were hunting Malone and Harvey. No other connection has yet been found.' Loan paused to let this sink in. 'They all used aliases so how this gang, whoever they are, got their real names, I don't know.'

Not another mole in the station, I hope, Denison thought.

Denison spoke, 'Malone and his pal would appear to be suspects it would seem, even they are in prison.'

'They could still have worked through visitors, sir,' said D.C. Sam Potter.

'Phone the prison, Sam, and get a list of their visitors for the last five years that have been in. And their phone calls.'

'Yes, sir.'

'Emily, see what you can dig up on the six men: possible enemies, their contacts, et cetera.'

'Yes, sir,' replied D.C. Emily Young. 'Someone hated those guys pretty strongly to do what they did. I've never seen anything like it.'

'Yes, they did, and we need to take them out of circulation before they strike again,' said Denison. 'We may never get another informer after this.'

'Okay, let's go,' said Loan and the squad went to their computer workstations.

Denison began to write all they had so far up on an incident board. 'It's a start,' he muttered.

An hour later, Sam Potter took two sheets of paper from the printer. 'Sir, we've got the list of visitors those two have had in their prisons.' Harvey and Malone were incarcerated in separate prisons as they had mutually threatened to murder each other.

Denison took the sheets. 'Hmm, they don't seem to have been very popular. Just a handful of visitors each. We can leave the relatives out for the moment and concentrate on the unknowns. Hold on a second! There is the same bloke visiting both, several times: Montgomery Winston Burnside!'

'Monty Burnside! Now there's a name from the past. I've not heard that name in donkeys' years,' said Mary Loan.

'Well known safecracker and sadistic excuse for a human being back in the day, he was,' Denison said.

'Sounds like the type to cut off fingers for the fun of it,' D.C. Emily Young added.

'Right, get out there and find him, all of you,' Denison said firmly. 'He is our number one suspect as of now.'

Chapter Three

'Chummy has gone to ground, sir. Burnside that is,' said D.I. Loan the next day. 'No one has seen him for days. At least no one is talking. Cannot blame them, I suppose.'

'I suppose not,' Denison said. 'There must be a way of tracking him. Bank account if he has one. Withdrawals? He has to get cash wherever he is. Check a few of the main mobile phone providers and see if they have him as a customer.'

'No need, sir,' D.C. Potter chimed in. 'EE have him, and he is using his phone regularly…'

'Where?' asked Denison eagerly.

'In Lichfield, sir. Specifically, in Netherstowe.'

'There's a big hotel there if I remember correctly,' said Mary Loan.

'Grab your coats!' Denison said cheerily. 'Call Armed Response to meet us there in case he is armed.'

***

'I'm afraid Mr Harcourt, as he called himself, checked out yesterday, Chief Inspector,' said the hotel receptionist, Glen Cartwright. He had identified Burnside from a mugshot. 'He paid cash so I did not query the name.'

'Darn it. Should have guessed Burnside would move about,' Denison said angrily.

'But I do have his car registration number for our car park checks if it helps,' the receptionist said raising an eyebrow. 'He left a forwarding address but it's probably false.'

'It certainly may be, young man,' Denison grinned. Cartwright wrote the number and address down and handed it to Denison.

Back in their car, Loan checked the number with Vehicle Registration HQ. 'According to their records that number is of a car scrapped three years ago after a fire. The address does not exist.'

'Foiled again. Why is everything against us?' Denison sounded frustrated. 'But I suppose police work would be boring if it were easy. Okay, back to Castlewood.'

'Shall I keep checking his bank withdrawals from the cash machines, sir?' Emily Young asked.

'Yes, of course. Though if he has any sense he will quit.'

'Circulate his photo to all hotels in the county and all police stations. Warn them that he may be armed.'

Days went by with nothing new turning up. Denison paced up and down like a caged tiger. He thumped a meaty fist into his other palm.

'Sir, do you think a television broadcast would help?' asked D.I. Loan.

'I suppose it might. I detest doing those. I'm no movie actor and I don't have the looks!'

Mary Loan almost giggled but managed to keep a straight face. 'Erm, shall I contact them, sir? They had been seeking an interview just after the murders.'

'Yes, do that. I had better shave,' Denison rubbed the stubble on his chin.

A few hours later, a TV crew from ITN arrived and set up their cameras.

'Right then, Chief Inspector, if you would sit in the middle seat at the table, and your colleagues either side,' said the interviewer.

'Be sure to get my better side,' Denison joked. *Does he have one?* the interviewer thought.

'Right, all ready? When I say "action", we go live. Three, two, one and…action!' said the camera director.

'Today, we have with us Detective Chief Inspector Denison of the Staffordshire Constabulary,' the interviewer began. 'Viewers will no doubt have heard of the heinous murders of six men in Castlewood some days ago. Chief Inspector, what help are you seeking from the British public today?'

Denison cleared his throat and trying to look confident, said, 'Six men were kidnapped and brutally tortured before a gang shot them. As yet we do not know how many were in this gang, but we are seeking one particular individual.' He paused while a photo of Montgomery Burnside was shown on screen.

'We have reason to believe this man, Montgomery Burnside, a local man, participated in this crime. If any member of the public has knowledge of the whereabouts of this man, please contact Crimestoppers or dial 999, or any police station. This man is dangerous and on no account should members of the public approach him.' Denison glanced at the interviewer.

'Thank you, Chief Inspector. Remember, viewers, do not approach this person. Call the police or Crimestoppers. Their number is on your screen.'

'Well, that went very well, Denison,' said the Chief Superintendent when the cameras stopped.

'Thank you, sir. I've never been so nervous. I'm not cut out for this sort of thing,' Denison replied. He mopped sweat from his brow.

'Nonsense, old chap, you did splendidly. Very professional if I may say,' said the interviewer. *Less of the old,* Denison thought. He smiled and nodded.

'Well, we shall be off, guys. We've another shoot, no pun intended, lined up in Birmingham,' the interviewer continued.

'Yes, and thank you all,' said Denison.

***

D.I. Loan said, 'The phones have been going crazy, sir, since your TV appearance. Burnside has been seen everywhere from Glasgow to Brighton.'

'Hmm, probably mostly crank calls, but get the local cops to check them out, Mary. Especially the local sightings. We may be lucky and nab him.'

Two days later: 'Sir, great news. Burnside has been lifted by our uniform colleagues in Norwich. He was hiding out in a bed and breakfast,' said D.C. Emily Young. 'They are bringing him here.'

'Great news, indeed,' said Denison. 'Get him in the interview room as soon as he gets here. I want to hear what he has to say.'

Burnside was hustled into the interview room past the press reporters who had somehow got wind of his capture. *So much for security,* Denison thought.

'Right then, Burnside, for the tape, where were you on the day the six men were murdered here in Castlewood?' Denison asked.

Burnside looked at him, looking puzzled. 'What six men?'

'Six men who were tortured and shot by you and your accomplices.'

'Don't know anything about them. It wasn't me and I don't have accomplices, neither,' Burnside replied with a grin.

'Where were you that day, the twenty-fifth of March?'

'The twenty-fifth of March? Let me think.' He looked at the ceiling and rubbed his chin thoughtfully. 'Oh, now I remember. Try asking your "Old Bill" colleagues in Stafford.' He grinned from ear to ear.

'Why Stafford?' Denison asked.

'Because, Inspector, I was detained for D and D the previous night and all that day. At the magistrate's court, I was. Got fined a hundred quid, didn't I?' He laughed. 'That's drunk and disorderly in case you don't know.'

Denison ignored the quip and asked D.I. Loan to check with the Stafford police station. *Pity they had not thought to inform us,* Denison thought.

When she returned, Loan said that what Burnside had claimed was true. He had been in custody all day.

'Right, that lets you off being actually at the scene, but you could have been pulling the strings. You had been visiting Malone and Harvey regularly this past five years. Why?' Denison asked.

'Because we are members of…we are members of the same, erm, chess club, aren't we?' Burnside smirked. 'Love a game of chess, we do.'

'Members of the same murder gang more like,' Denison said. Burnside shrugged. 'Did the three of you plot revenge on the six men?'

'Revenge, Inspector? Do you imply they were informers on my mates? Dear, dear, how awful.'

Smart lad, eh? Denison thought. 'Who were your accomplices? And why have you been in hiding since the crime?' Denison asked.

'Let me reiterate. I have no accomplices and I was in hiding because the "Bad Boys" gang in Manchester are looking for me on another matter, which I shall not detail. I'll put it this way: I'm a dead man if they get me, and now it will be all over the news that I am here. I demand police protection! I pay my taxes!'

'If I am satisfied that you are innocent, we will get you safely away. Now, tell us their names, the accomplices you say you don't have,' Denison was losing patience. He knew he had nothing substantial to connect Burnside to the crime.

'I have nothing further to say.' Burnside folded his arms and sat back in his chair. He yawned.

'All right, you can go, for the present, on the condition you contact us daily on a number D.I. Loan will give you, so we know where you are. Or we can put you in a safe house.'

'You have no right to make me phone,' Burnside protested.

'You asked for police protection. Either that or you will be at the mercy of that gang. We will come to your aid should they find you. A car will be in your vicinity at all times until this is over, or you can stay in a safe house. Your choice. And we have not forgotten about the fake car registration plates.'

'Okay, I'll phone you every day until you catch the real criminals,' said Burnside. He was then driven to a hotel and left there. An unmarked police car was parked nearby with two detectives from the squad on board.

'Do you think he is innocent, sir?' Loan asked.

'No, not really. But I do believe him when he says a gang is after him. He was scared. We need to get the others who did the murders and link them to him. I have a gut feeling he is involved, and my gut is rarely wrong,' Denison laughed, and he patted his stomach.

Chapter Four

Denison and Loan visited Sidney Malone in prison.

'Well, if it isn't Officer Dibble, erm, Denison. I am privileged,' Malone said sarcastically. He covered his mouth with a hand, yawned and then folded his arms.

'You know why we are here,' Denison said.

'Nope, why should I?' Malone replied.

'Because you plotted the deaths of six men you thought were informers. Six innocent men we had never heard of,' Denison said.

'Oh, indeed? Whether they were or not I had nothing to do with their deaths,' Malone leaned forward and stabbed a finger in Denison's direction. 'Nothing…at …all.'

'Your friend, Harvey, says different. He says you planned it all. You got Monty Burnside to set it up. Didn't you?' Denison was bluffing but looked Malone in the eyes.

'Harvey is no friend of mine. And he is only trying to save his own skin. Once again, I had nothing to do with any murders. How could I, me being locked up in here?'

'You could be locked up for the rest of your life when we prove your guilt, Malone. We shall leave you—for the moment.' Denison and Loan then left him and went to the prison Harvey was in.

***

'Right then, Harvey, I'll come straight to the point,' Denison said. 'Malone has implied that you organised the murders of six men you think informed on you some five years ago. What have you to say?'

'What six men? I know nothing about no murders, Denison. Nor a dickey bird. No way, José. How could I do that from in here?' He waved an arm around the room.

'Through your mutual friend Monty Burnside, that's how.'

'Nonsense, Inspector. All we chatted about on his visits was family and football and stuff like that. If Monty did these murders, and I doubt it very much, then it was his own doing or Malone organised it. I'm just trying to serve my time.'

'We will prove you were involved, and you will spend the rest of your life in here,' Denison stood, and the two detectives left. Harvey looked worried.

***

Back in his office, Denison was discussing matters with his staff when there was a tap on the door to the corridor, and a head peered in. 'Hope you don't mind the intrusion,' said Superintendent Harris.

'Not at all, sir,' Denison said. 'Do come in. Take a seat.' Harris sat down when another detective vacated his chair.

'How are things progressing in the six murders' case? I hear you have Burnside being guarded.'

'Yes, sir, he is reporting daily as to where he is staying. He is, of course, being followed if he leaves the premises, and

166

any visitors are being checked out. So far only his brother has contacted him.'

'The brother is clear? What about phone calls?' asked Harris.

'Yes, sir, the brother has no record. He is a clergyman in fact, local Baptist church, and the hotel is listing any calls he makes from his room. So far he has only called the brother and his bank.'

'Hmm, good show. I suppose it is best to keep him safe, at least until he is beyond suspicion. We must find the guilty person or persons, Denison. The press are breathing down my neck.'

'Yes, sir,' said Denison.

'Well, I'll leave you to it. Continue with the excellent work.'

Off to play golf, no doubt, Denison thought. 'Thank you, sir,' he said, and smiled.

'Right, gang, let's review what we have in this case, shall we?' Denison continued when his boss had left.

D.S. Sandra Johnston said, 'Burnside is still under observation, sir. There are reports of known gang members asking questions about him in local pubs. They are definitely after his blood.'

'Mary, put another car on surveillance where he is now. Where is he by the way?'

Mary Loan replied, 'He is in a small hotel in Lichfield, sir, the "Ye Olde Three Spires Inn".'

'Hmm, better inform the local constabulary we are operating there, but don't say why. Don't want some zealous P.C. blowing our cover. Okay, get digging, troops. These criminals won't catch themselves.'

The questioning of all locals who were engaged in crime to a greater or lesser extent continued. No one knew anything, or they were keeping their heads down.

Chapter Five

The investigations were getting nowhere fast. D.C.I. Denison spent his evenings at home, going over things in his head but produced no clues at all.

'What are we missing, Millicent?' he asked his wife.

'How should I know, Dear? You're the detective,' she replied, grinning.

'I know, I know; it was a rhetorical question,' he laughed.

'Tell you what: you can smoke your pipe, just this once, while I prepare supper. It might give you inspiration.'

'Thank you, my dear,' and Denison produced pipe and tobacco. 'Where are the matches?' He looked around in desperation. 'Ah, the cat's lying on them. Scram, you furball.' Cedric the cat was unceremoniously pushed off the couch and made his way to the kitchen, looking annoyed. He soon perked up when his other human produced a box of "Catty Crunchies".

Denison lit up and settled back enjoying the unaccustomed luxury of a pipe in his own home. However, even after a second fill, nothing had come to him.

'May as well go to bed,' he said to his wife. 'Perhaps I shall dream of something.' He yawned.

'Yes, you do that, Dear, and I shall be up when I have tidied up these supper dishes.' Roast beef sandwiches and decaf tea had been consumed with relish.

Denison spent a restless night. Millicent was forced to resort to the spare bed in another room.

'No ideas come to you, my dear?' she asked over breakfast.

'Nothing. What have I missed? It's so frustrating,' Denison sighed.

'Get all your staff together and brainstorm until you get a solution. After all, if, as the song says, "Twa heids are better than yin,"' she tried her best Scot's accent, 'surely all you lot are better still!'

'Yes, you are right as always, my genius wife. I'll do just that.' He kissed her on the cheek and set off for the office, having emailed all the detectives to be there at half past nine without fail.

***

'After all these weeks, we have found no one for those murders. So, we are going to stay here and brainstorm until we get a solution.' Shocked and worried faces were on all the detectives.

'You mean, like, all day, sir?' one man, D.C. Caden Moggs, known as Moggie, ventured to ask.

'And all night if need be. I have arranged regular coffee and food supplies, and toilet breaks of course as and when needed.' Groans all round.

Everyone settled down as comfortably as the office furniture would permit. Silence ensued. Neckties were loosened or removed.

'To kick things off, sir,' said D.I. Mary Loan, 'I shall go over what we do know, if I may?' Denison nodded assent. She approached the incident board. 'The murders took place on Saturday March twenty-fifth at 23, Marston Crescent, Castlewood.' Everyone nodded.

'There were six victims, all of whom had been tortured, mutilated and shot or strangled. Presumably, the killers used a silencer. The only connection found so far that links the six men is that they were all informers in the Malone/Harvey case five years ago.'

'But are they not still locked up?' commented D.C. Sam Potter.

'Yes, Sam, that is correct. We checked their records of visitors and phone calls, and the only person common to both was this character,' she tapped a photograph with a pen, 'Montgomery Burnside, aka Monty.'

'The only problem is,' Denison interrupted, 'he has a solid, cast-iron alibi…unfortunately, he was locked up at the time.' The others chuckled at Denison's disgusted expression.

'So, has anyone any bright ideas?' asked Loan. 'We'll have a short break to give us time to think.' Everyone made a beeline for the coffee machine.

Ten minutes later, Denison said, 'Right, back to work. You may finish your coffees as we speak. Has anyone a thought on this?' Silence. Everyone took a sudden interest in the ceiling.

'Sir, perhaps we are barking up the wrong tree. What if it is only a coincidence the six victims were associated with Malone?' Sandra Johnston asked.

'I don't believe in coincidences,' said Denison. 'But we shall keep in mind the possibility.'

D.I. Loan said, 'We cannot find another case where all six were involved, sir. Two or three maybe but not all six. Could they have fallen foul of some gang for another reason?'

'Yes, quite possibly,' Denison said. 'But who and where from?'

'Sir,' said D.C. Young, 'that gang from Burton-upon-Trent, the "Trent Tigers" they call themselves…'

'Yeah, they are a bad lot and no mistake,' said Sam Potter.

Emily Young resumed, 'Well, they have been known to chop off fingers and such in the past. It is a sort of trademark so to speak.'

'Hmm, you're right, Emily. What's-his-name? "Chopper" Harrison, first name Colin, is a member if I remember right,' Denison said. 'Get him in for questioning. Should have thought of that character before. With any luck, we could have solved this case.'

Chapter Six

Colin Harrison was duly rounded up and taken to an interview room.

'Oi, copper, why am I here? I have done nothing, well, not recently anyway,' he sat back with a smug look on his face. A face with eyes too close together, a large square jaw and an overly large mouth. Thick black eyebrows and a huge nose completed the visage.

'You are here to aid us in our enquiries, Mr Harrison,' said Denison in his most pleasant voice. 'As you know, I'm sure, six local men were violently attacked and murdered recently and as you have a history as long as my arm of such violent attacks, we feel you may have been involved.' Denison sat back and stared at Harrison.

'Me? No way. That has nothing to do with me. Not a thing. When was it anyway?'

'On the twenty-fifth of March,' D.I. Loan added.

'Well, sorry to disappoint you, Officers, but Yours Truly was on holiday in bonny Scotland at the time. Spot of fishing. Lovely it was, snow, fresh air. Very bracing it was. Didn't like the grub much though.'

'How long did you stay?' Denison asked.

'A week. From the twenty-second, for a week, in a little hotel,' Harrison smiled.

'This hotel have a name?' asked Loan.

'The, what was it? Yes, "The Deerstalker". That's what it is called. "The Deerstalker". You can check it out.'

'We'll check it out, don't worry,' Denison said. 'You may go, but don't leave the country.'

'Thank you. I have no intention of going anywhere,' Harrison smirked.

When they were alone, Denison said, 'Mary, check out his alibi. Email his photo to Scotland and ask them to get the hotel staff to identify him.'

'Yes, sir. He sounds too sure of his alibi to be lying, I'm afraid,' Mary Loan said.

'I know. Still, best checked out anyway,' Denison sighed. He was beginning to lose hope of solving the case.

***

'Sir,' D. I. Loan said later, 'His alibi checks out. Seems he was definitely in Scotland at the time of the murders.'

'Just as I feared,' Denison replied. 'I was sure we had our man, so, we're back to square one.'

'We just seem to be hitting a series of brick walls, sir. Someone did the killings. Perhaps it is a gang from some other city. A gang that, for some reason, wanted the six men dead.'

'Possibly, Mary. Let's keep searching the backgrounds of the victims: who they associated with, where they socialised, that sort of thing,' Denison added.

Days passed without anything new turning up. No DNA evidence was found at the murder scene when every surface had been tested. The detectives concluded that the murderers had worn overalls and probably masks and hoods.

D.C. Sam Potter was with the rest of the squad as they gathered around the incident board, 'Sir, I have just been to Stoke at a football match with some mates, and I am certain I saw that Colin Harrison in the crowd. Unfortunately, my phone's battery was flat so I couldn't film him. I tried to get nearer but the crowd started to leave, and I lost sight of him.'

'But he is under surveillance **here** in Castlewood,' Denison stated firmly.

'That is what I was thinking, sir,' Potter said. 'He cannot have been in two places at once.'

'Get on to the surveillance team and check it out, Sam.'

Potter did so and ten minutes later, he reported, 'Sir, they are adamant that Harrison never left his house.'

'So, are you certain that it was Harrison?' Denison asked Potter.

'Yes, sir, as sure as I'm standing here,' Potter replied. 'They had eyeball on him frequently.'

'Unless he has a…' D.I. Loan began.

'Twin?!' said Potter emphatically.

'Haul Harrison in here, **at once**. We'll get to the bottom of this,' Denison thumped a fist into his other palm.

Chapter Seven

'Well, Mr Harrison, we meet again,' Denison said.

'Looks like it, Officer. I have already told you that I was in Scotland in March, skiing and stuff. Nearly broke a leg, I did.'

'Are you quite certain about that because our information tells us something different?'

Harrison was beginning to wonder just how much the police knew. 'Yes, very certain: as sure as night follows day and I follow Arsenal.' He grinned.

'Arsenal? Well, I suppose no one is perfect,' Denison said with a grin. 'Getting back to the matter in hand, we know it was not you in Scotland.'

'How do you figure that? I was there for a week. I told you that before,' Harrison stated once again. He sighed.

'Or could it have been someone impersonating you? Someone like…'

Harrison went pale. *He must know something,* he thought. 'You are only fishing, Denison. It was me. No one else.'

'Were you in Stoke recently at a football match?'

'Erm, no. I've been here since we last spoke. Never left the house.'

'Yes, my officers verified that, but who was it who was seen in Stoke? One of my men saw you, or someone who looks like you.'

Harrison was sweating profusely. 'He was mistaken. I have not been in Stoke in years.'

'You have a brother, don't you? A twin, in fact?' D.I. Loan interjected.

'No! No, I do not!'

'It is only a matter of time before… Oh, this may be him now,' said Denison as a knock came to the door. 'Enter!'

'Excuse me, sir, but the gentleman you were seeking has arrived, albeit reluctantly,' said a constable.

A scruffy individual shuffled through the door. He was identical to his brother except for two days' growth of beard.

'So, Mr Harrison, Colin that is, I assume you know your twin,' Denison raised his eyebrows.

'Yeah, okay. This is my brother Jeremy. But he had nothing to do with the murders either.'

'Jeremy, take a seat,' said Denison. He sat down. 'Your brother arranged a little holiday for you in Scotland. Is that correct?'

'Yeah, he did. It was a wedding anniversary present for me and the missus. Why?' Jeremy replied.

'Because we believe he, Colin, wanted an alibi for when he participated in six murders, Jeremy,' Mary Loan said.

Jeremy's mouth gaped. 'Six murders?! No way!'

'It's true,' said Denison. 'Background checks on the victims brought up an interesting fact: all owed your brother a great deal of money for betting. Colin then discovered they were grassing to us about a certain gang, the "Trent Tigers".

Between them, they kidnapped the men, tortured them just for amusement, then shot them.'

Jeremy went pale and almost was sick. 'I…I know nothing of this. Nothing! It was just a holiday as I have said. I find it difficult to believe my brother, my twin brother, would do that. It can't be true.'

'You booked into the hotel under his name,' Denison continued.

'Yeah, so what? Colin had it in his name so to avoid confusion he told me to go under his name…No! No. There must be a reason, an explanation,' Jeremy cried as he realised what had happened. 'I've been a fool. Colin, tell him there is a good explanation. Tell him!'

Colin remained silent.

'So,' Denison said, 'Colin Harrison, it would seem you had every opportunity to carry out the murders. You will be remanded in custody until your trial for multiple homicides. Mary, charge him with murder. If we find that Malone and Harvey were involved, they will be behind bars for life.'

'Yes, sir.'

Malone and Harvey were not found to be involved, at least no connection was found.

Denison thought to himself, *I am certain Malone and Harvey are involved. I can feel it in my gut. When they are released I'll have a tail put on them and see what crops up.*

He lifted a phone and spoke to the Governors of the prisons where they were being held.

The End

Milton Keynes UK
Ingram Content Group UK Ltd.
UKHW022233081223
434043UK00012B/535

9 781398 477094